For Emma

LET DOWN YOUR HAIR

Orion

Bryony Gordon

ORION CHILDREN'S BOOKS

First published in Great Britain in 2022 by Hodder & Stoughton

1 3 5 7 9 10 8 6 4 2

Text copyright © Bryony Gordon, 2022

The moral rights of the author have been asserted.

*All characters and events in this publication, other than those clearly
in the public domain, are fictitious and any resemblance to
real persons, living or dead, is purely coincidental.*

A CIP catalogue record for this book is available from the British Library.

ISBN 978 1 510 10747 2

Typeset in Goudy Old Style by Avon DataSet Ltd, Alcester, Warwickshire

Printed and bound in Great Britain by Clays Ltd, Elcograf S.p.A.

The paper and board used in this book
are made from wood from responsible sources.

Orion Children's Books
An imprint of
Hachette Children's Group
Part of Hodder & Stoughton Limited
Carmelite House
50 Victoria Embankment
London EC4Y 0DZ

An Hachette UK Company
www.hachette.co.uk
www.hachettechildrens.co.uk

CHAPTER 1

When Barb found the thing that would change her life forever, she felt strangely calm.

Blissed out even.

Like everything suddenly made perfect sense.

And nothing had ever made perfect sense to Barb. It hadn't even made *imperfect* sense.

When her fingers came across it, she felt a jolt of electricity run through her body, a jolt that was familiar to her from all the times at school Serena and Jess had honed in to view, their vicious snarls trained on her. It was the kind of jolt your body normally gives you to warn you that something bad is about to happen – it made Barb feel as though her stomach was crammed in her throat, her head was about to float off and her knees were going to buckle.

But that day in her room, when the jolt came, Barb was alone. She was safe. She had not seen Jess or Serena for

1

months – or rather, they hadn't seen her. Which was just the way she liked it. She had watched them out of her bedroom window, strutting through the estate to school or huddled conspiratorially on the swings in the largely vandalised playground, imagining bitchy comments spewing out of their mouths like speech bubbles above their heads. But they had not seen her. It wasn't just that she was too high up for them to see – it was also that they wouldn't have bothered to look.

Today, like every other day, she was no longer at school; she was alone in her tower with only her phone and her two-hundred thousand ShowReal followers for company.

The day had started like any other: drab, dreary, dull, the universe providing no special clues to the curveball it was about to throw her. Barb woke up in her room to the sounds on the street below of children brawling. Even twelve flights up, their noise carried – she had stopped having to set the alarm on her phone. Not that she needed an alarm any more; not since she had walked out of school six months earlier for the last time, a clutch of crappy GCSEs in her pocket and her head held low.

She had read books about grief where people would have a few precious seconds when they woke up, precious seconds where they thought everything was normal, before reality caught up with them and their worlds came crashing down again. But Barb didn't know normal. Barb didn't know anything other than waking up to the low-level loss that had squatted there on her chest since she was old enough to remember. When she opened her eyes, she sometimes let out a bleak cackle at what greeted her.

Her days were all the same. She would wander into the living room to find Sorcha had gone to work, a note on the coffee table reminding her what she had to do that day in terms of content and posts and *creation*. Then she would stare out of the window at the laundry fluttering on the balcony – it was more a death trap than an area from which to enjoy some sunshine – and wonder what life was like beyond it.

Barb lived in a tower block in south London, but sometimes she felt like she woke up in some budget version of a Kardashian's home. The plastic peonies in a tall vase from TK Maxx might look real with a good angle on them, but on closer inspection appeared to have fallen straight off a factory line, faulty. On the walls were prints that her aunt Sorcha had framed and hung, featuring the kind of inspirational quotes that went down a storm on social media but made her cringe in real life. 'If opportunity doesn't knock, build the door' or 'Life is not about waiting for the storm to pass, but learning to dance in the rain', and her least favourite of all: 'Shoot for the moon – if you miss you will still land among the stars.'

The thing was, with only a direct view of another tower block from her bedroom window, Barb couldn't actually see the sky, let alone the moon or the stars, just the balconies full of laundry, rusting bikes and pot plants.

Her bed had been 'gifted' by a home furnishing brand in exchange for a video on 'easy at home bedroom style'. On camera, with a good filter, it looked like it had a velvet headboard. In the cold light of day, it had the texture of a cheap knock-off velour tracksuit. It took up most of her tiny room so she had to be clever with camera angles – which was lucky, because camera angles were almost the only thing she was clever at.

The room screamed influencer. Barb hated it. She felt sure it wasn't her, even if she hadn't a clue who *her* was. Her favourite corner was the one hidden by the bedroom door, where a pile of dirty laundry grew out of sight of any cameras.

The rest of the flat was definitely not like this. Barb's bedroom was the only room that Sorcha had made any effort with – not out of familial love, but because it was where Barb produced all the content for her platforms, and she couldn't beam to her 200k followers from the breeze block surrounds of the living room, where from almost every angle you could see the unironic sixties architecture of the Warriner Estate.

She stared out at the slate-grey sky while spooning mushy

cereal into her mouth. Out of the corner of her eye, a stray strand of her hair sparkled in the harsh overhead lights of the living room, a reminder of her potential. In front of Barb lay the whole of the world – or the whole of her world, at least – in the form of the estate.

There were more than six hundred flats spread over six buildings that sometimes felt more like cell blocks. These cell blocks had been plonked in an apparently haphazard way around an area of concrete and weeds that she supposed, at one point, someone in the council had thought would create an air of community. There was a token nod at a playground, which all the local toddlers turned their noses up at on account of the fact that there was a much better, not to mention bigger, adventure playground a ten-minute walk away in the local park. In London, as on social media, there was *always* something much better around the corner.

The estate jostled for space with some luxury new builds across the road that had panoramic views of the river, as opposed to the odd murky view of it through other buildings enjoyed on the Warriner Estate. Sorcha loved those flats. She had once even tried to get Barb to come with her to a viewing and pretend to be buyers, but Barb couldn't bear the thought of being spotted and giving any more ammunition to Serena and Jess, who already thought she was a stuck-up cow who fancied herself as above them.

In fact the only way Barb was above them was physically,

living as she did on a higher floor of the estate than they did. In all other ways, she knew she was well below them.

While the possibilities for Barb seemed limitless online, elsewhere they had been stunted for some time. Her life existed almost entirely within the flat, and more specifically within the screen of her iPhone. If she climbed to the top of the block and looked out the window on a clear day, she could see in the distance all sorts of things on the skyline – the looming towers of Battersea Power Station, the bubbles of the London Eye, and the huge jagged glass rock that was the Shard – the place she and Jess had dreamed of celebrating their sixteenth birthdays.

Though she had lived in this city her whole life, she had barely been to any of these places. Her childhood had been spent playing with Jess on the estate and in the local park. But when Jess had cut her dead and the social media thing had taken off, her world had narrowed even more, until now the most exciting place Barb ever found herself in was the cupboard-sized kitchen, eating her Weetabix.

One thing Barb was grateful for was that the day was not a hair-washing day – a seemingly simple process, but one that could take aeons given the length and thickness of her strawberry-blonde hair. It trailed down to her waist, so substantial and heavy that it sometimes felt like she was taking another entity entirely into the shower with her.

As she got dressed in clothes that anybody else would wear to a bar for drinks – spray-on jeans, silver platforms, a brightly coloured shirt – Barb tried not to consider that she was not, in fact, anybody else, and that on the balance of probabilities, she would never wear this outfit – or any other outfit – to a bar for drinks. She would probably not wear it anywhere outside the flat.

Like everything else in her life, it was all for show.

In her bedroom, she placed the camera tripod on her dressing table, and carefully positioned her iPhone in it so that it would capture the most flattering angles and avoid the dirty laundry. As she switched the ring light on – used to give her a flattering glow so that she was not reliant on filters – she squinted to adjust her eyes to the brightness. Then she brushed out her hair meticulously to ensure it didn't look like she had just got out of bed.

Today she was doing a twisted updo, a variation on a simple style that her followers could not get enough of. She could brush her hair all day and her followers could not get enough of it. She tried not to think about the troll accounts that had begun to show a real interest in her recently – the troll accounts she would have been sure belonged to Serena if another voice in her head didn't chastise her for being arrogant enough to think that Serena would waste her time and energy doing such a thing.

7

Sometimes the voices in her head were the only other ones Barb would hear for days and days.

She took a deep breath, pressed record on her phone, and began. Barb could do these complicated hairstyles with her eyes closed. Sometimes she did actually close her eyes as she separated and braided her hair, or made silly faces that the camera couldn't see. It gave her pleasure to know that while thousands of viewers watched the back of her head, at the front of it, she was screwing up her face to do her best impression of a gargoyle. People weren't interested in her face, or her expressions, or the thoughts contained inside her – they just wanted to see the back of her head, and sometimes the front, but only to note how she put a curling tong through her hair, or the angle at which she coated herself in hairspray.

She was dexterous as hell, and there was no part of her scalp that she hadn't got mapped out in her head. She knew exactly how to position a braid, where to place a bobby pin. She could blow-dry and style her hair as well as any of the most experienced and talented staff members at a high-end salon. She couldn't form a lasting friendship, and the teachers at school had never even thought of mentioning university to her. But with her hair, she could turn even a blue rinse or a perm into a piece of magic.

The twisted updo was, despite its name, pretty straightforward, and Barb was thinking more about the editing she would do later when the jolt came.

When the red alert sounded.

She was creating a hidden bit of volume at the crown of her head when she felt it.

One moment there was hair, hair, hair – a little bit greasy given that wash day was approaching – and the next moment nothing but skin, skin, skin.

A small patch of it, almost perfectly naked, right below the centre of her crown.

Her breath caught as she felt the jolt. She inhaled and exhaled deeply as she began to rub her fingers along the smooth, soft skin. And then the familiar rush of adrenaline gave way to something far more alien to her: a sort of calm that dropped over her body as she continued to stroke the back of her head. She felt strangely comforted. It was almost *relaxing*.

Only her iPhone was able to tell her how long she had sat there transfixed by this new sensation at the back of her head. She had been in a four-minute-long daydream, switching from the naked scalp to the hair over and over again, as if she had found her own private world within the familiar walls of the flat.

A sudden wail of sirens outside brought Barb back to reality. She shook her head, abandoned the twisted updo and the filming, and took her iPhone to her bed where she sat, cross-legged, gripped by the footage she had captured.

It was there, as bold as brass: a bald patch, like a tiny white island in the seemingly never-ending sea of her hair. She paused the video and wondered what it could possibly be, what it could possibly mean, and where it could possibly have come from. She checked the back of her head again just to make sure the patch hadn't disappeared in the intervening moments: that it hadn't all been a dream.

It was still there: smooth and warm and *secret*.

Barb decided then and there that she would keep this to herself, nurture it like a precious treasure. At last, here was something that she knew about herself that nobody else did.

CHAPTER 2

SIX MONTHS AGO

On the day that marked her sixteenth birthday, Barb McDonnell woke up with more bounce inside her body and brain than she had experienced in the entire 5,839 days that had preceded it. It was not because she had some marvellous party planned, or even because she expected a mountain of presents – more of a molehill, if that – but because it was her last day of school. Ever.

Ever, ever, *ever*.

Barb had dreamt about this day for . . . oooh, her entire life really, but her estrangement from Jess had intensified her longing to get the hell out of Queenstown Academy and away from anyone even vaguely associated with it.

As she bounded out of bed, Barb thought triumphantly, *Goodbye, Serena, you and your shade won't be missed! Laters, Jess, your face slapped with bitterness like the thick foundation your favourite MUA uses! You can all kiss my ass, which will be breaking the internet about the same time you're all starting to study for your tedious A Levels and NVQs!*

She would never say these things out loud because a) who would be listening? and b) who would be listening?

Not her aunt, who had already left for work, or body blast, or whatever it was that motivated her to be up and out of the flat during the dead zone that was 6 a.m.

Even today, Barb's birthday and last day at school, Sorcha had not bothered to hang around or serve her a celebratory breakfast in bed. Not that Barb really wanted to wake up and immediately see her aunt's preposterously contoured face (other things Barb silently thought but never, ever said: with that palette, is my aunt trying to turn her cheekbones into a mountain range to rival the Himalayas?), but a note would have been nice. A birthday card even. An acknowledgement of her *existence*.

Still, Barb wasn't going to let this get her down. Today was the first day of the rest of her life, and she had decided that it was going to be an outrageously good life. It was going to be the kind of life that others only dreamed of. That she had dreamed of, now she came to think about it, ever since she and Jess had started watching toy-unboxing videos on YouTube, way back in year four.

It was a hot June day, the kind that melted tarmac and temperaments, the kind that Barb hated because it was so hard to hide from the harsh glare of the inner-city sun. Tarmac melted, heat rose, and up on the twelfth floor of the Warriner Estate, boy did Barb know it. That morning she had done away with the fancy dress of her online life and put on the armour for her offline one: school uniform and hair scraped back off her face into a bun – as inconspicuous as was possible with all her locks. Head low, with the knowledge that if things got really bad, she could shake out the bun and hide her burning cheeks behind her hair.

They were taking their final GCSE that morning, in the stuffy, intimidating school hall. Despite the oppressive heat and the seriousness of the task ahead of them, the head teacher had decreed that windows were to be kept shut to keep out the noise of the rest of the school. Instead, large fans had been placed at the back and front of the hall, but they had little effect other than to blow the hot air into the middle of the room, which was where Barb found herself sitting that day – at a desk that wobbled every time she put pen to paper which, fortunately for those around her, wasn't very often.

In the queue to enter the maths exam, Jess and Serena had been excitedly discussing their plans for the evening. They were going to The Secret Garden, the pub at the bottom of the estate where you could drink booze without anybody asking for proof of age. Barb had done her best not to listen, instead reciting her candidate number over and over again in her head, like a meditation to keep away the jolts: *nine–six–one–three, nine–six–one–three, nine–six–one–three*. In two hours' time she would be free of this school, free of the horror of these corridors, free of the electric-shock existence that had come to characterise her life there.

Thanks to her hair, she didn't have to do well in this exam – or any of her exams, for that matter – she just had to do them. Legally. So that Sorcha didn't get arrested. Beyond that, she had no interest in her GCSEs. She would not be nervously awaiting the results in two months' time. She would not be choosing her A levels based on her results, or picking an NVQ. She was going full-time on ShowReal, and she reminded herself that this was a good thing despite what Jess and Serena said.

Sure, it would mean she would become an adult with almost no useful qualifications, save perhaps for an art GCSE. But it also meant that she could get the hell out of school and focus on creating any life she dreamed of online. Or any life her *aunt* had dreamed of for her. And even that had to be better than this one.

For most of the exam, the only numbers Barb interacted with were the ones on the clock at the front of the hall. She drew some doodles on her paper and took a cursory glance through the questions, thinking it would be rude not to.

14

She could answer most of them – she was not stupid, no matter what anyone said – but what would have been the point? Doing well in her GCSEs would only have encouraged her teachers to persuade her to stay on for sixth form, and she had worked hard over the years at secondary school to dampen their enthusiasm for her academic life – mostly by *not* working hard at her academic life.

'She has such potential,' various teachers had told her aunt back at the beginning of school, but even then Sorcha had only really been interested in Barb's hair and the potential it might have to earn them money.

The seconds and minutes ticked by and Barb watched her classmates as they sat in their own sweat and stress, believing that their whole lives were predicated on this one exam. Deep down in her soul, Barb envied them. Most of them had parents they wanted to make proud; they had careers they wanted to make happen; they had friends they wanted to be able to discuss the intricacies of the exam with later. Barb had only her two-hundred thousand followers, and none of them would give a stuff how she did in her GCSEs. They just wanted to know how to create beach-hair perfect waves, or how to fake volume. No, the only thing Barb needed to please was the algorithm.

As she pondered this, Barb hadn't realised she was looking in Jess's direction. So when Jess looked up and around at her, they caught each other's eye. For the briefest of moments, Barb allowed her brain to run away from her, to a place where Jess hadn't turned into a complete bitch, to a place where she wanted to check in with her oldest friend and see how she was doing on her last day of school. On her *birthday*.

There was no way Jess would have forgotten it, because this was the first that they hadn't spent together, making one of their jokey birthday-present-unboxing videos in the style of the YouTuber they had adored when they were eight. They had watched her videos for hours, until they turned eleven and realised it was a bit weird that a grown woman was making a career out of collecting L.O.L. Surprise! dolls. But they had kept up their habit of filming their own unboxing videos on each of their birthdays, when they would sarcastically play at unwrapping the usually pathetic present they had been gifted by their respective adults, imagining what it would be like if, one day, they could actually be like the YouTubers who got paid to unwrap gifts every day.

Barb remembered looking at Jess on her last birthday, cheeks still wet from the latest bout of hysterics they'd had. It had been caused by a well-intended gift from Jess's gran.

'A knitted toilet-roll holder? A KNITTED TOILET-ROLL HOLDER?' Barb had squealed as she brandished a garishly coloured doll complete with flouncy skirts.

'With those skirts – and that monobrow – your gran seems to have sent you a version of Frida Kahlo to stare at while you're weeing!'

Jess had let out a strangled shriek at the thought, then collapsed into yet more giggles.

'Let's always do this, Jess, eh?' Barb had suddenly said. 'Every birthday. Until we're ancient.'

Jess had looked back at her friend. 'TOTALLY ancient. Like, forty or something.'

To the girls' horror, Pete, Jess's dad, had suddenly called from the other room: 'Oi, do you mind? I'M FORTY!' Which had only inspired another round of hysterical shrieking from the girls.

But as it turned out, their fifteenth birthdays would be their last together.

Barb still had the video from Jess's birthday but she doubted very much that Jess had the content from hers. She'd seen how Jess spent her sixteenth birthday the month before, thanks to the endless carousel of screamingly 'fun!' pictures of the night in question that Serena had dumped on her ShowReal grid.

Barb had scrolled through them with an increasing sense of sadness – that was *her* friend, and those were things that *they* used to do together! – which crescendoed into a sort of hard-boiled rage when she got to the image of Jess and Serena having drinks at the top of the Shard. That had been where she and Jess had promised to go together as a joint sixteenth birthday celebration. But instead, Jess was living that dream with Serena while Barb was wondering if her aunt was going to remember to buy her a birthday card.

Was Jess softening now? Had she glanced in Barb's direction as a sort of conciliatory gesture on her birthday? Nope. Jess's icy glare quickly snapped Barb out of her daydream. Even now, in this exam hall, with everyone concentrating on their papers, Barb had made the mistake of not keeping her head low. She looked down and pretended to attempt a quadratic equation.

It was a relief when the invigilator called time. Barb hurried to get her things together – the pointless calculator, the barely used pen – and hoped she could make an exit without encountering Jess or Serena. But Jess was two rows in front of her, Serena two behind. As they stood to leave, she saw them catch each other's eyes over her head, giving each other a smile and Barb a sneer. Not for the first time, she felt like piggy in the middle. As they filed out of the hall and into the corridor, Barb pulled down her hair to cover her face. It was the wrong thing to do.

'Look at Miss La-Di-Da, showing off her silky, perfect locks,' sang Serena, tunelessly.

Barb lowered her head further, so that all she could see was the dirty grey floor and her scuffed Nikes on it. She began making her way quickly towards the door, towards the tantalising prospect of freedom.

She was nearly there, nearly there, near– Barb was stopped in her tracks by a burning sensation on her scalp. She realised with a start that someone was pulling her hair.

She was *sixteen years old, and someone was pulling her hair.*

She was not going to take this silently. She wasn't going to think something in her head but be too cowardly to say it out loud. This was her last day at school, the first day of her outrageously good life, and she was damned if she was going to let these absolute *asshats* make her feel like she was six years old.

'What?' she snapped suddenly from behind her fringe of hair, whirling round to face her attacker. 'WHAT DO YOU WANT FROM ME?'

Fellow students rushed by, so used to casual bullying that they barely even noticed it any more. Serena sniggered as Jess stood silently beside her. 'You think you're better than us, don't you?' she sneered. 'You think because you're leaving school for a life online that you're better than us, when in fact you're no more than a dumb wig that happens to be attached to a stupid body.' Jess still hadn't said anything but the look she gave Barb meant she didn't have to. Barb shook her head, turned, and started to walk away, towards the exit, towards the air, towards the beginning of her outrageously good life.

'You know you're *nothing* without your hair,' said Jess eventually, almost in a whisper. 'Nothing.'

The worst thing was, Barb did know it.

Barb was nothing without her hair, and she wasn't very much with it either. She felt sometimes just as Serena said – like a shop mannequin attached to a wig and little else, such was the obsession people had with the stuff that sprouted from her scalp. She had been born with a full head of hair so beautiful and unusual that the midwife had apparently held her aloft to gawp at her, a bit like Simba in *The Lion King*. 'Would you look at that!' she allegedly said, although Barb had been told this by Sorcha, who wasn't actually in the room at the time, so Barb was uncertain about its accuracy.

What *was* undisputed was that as everyone had been distracted by the newborn baby's hair – and perhaps if they hadn't been – no one noticed the eyes of the woman who had just given birth to her rolling back in her head, or the endless blood flowing from where the baby had just been removed. By the time it became clear that the new mother was in trouble, it was too late. It would have happened *anyway*, Sorcha always said, in a detached voice, about the terrible fate of her sister, Barb's mother. She had died of a hemorrhage. It was a freakish complication, a complete rarity, and Barb was not to feel bad about what had happened. It wasn't her fault.

Except, of course, it kind of was.

Though Barb had only been told the basics about her early days – her origins – she had imagined them in vivid Technicolor. She had painted life into her biological mother's face, and then watched it drain away as everyone fussed needlessly over the stupid baby hair on her stupid baby head. She had imagined CPR, a defibrillator, a dashing doctor applying paddles to her mother's chest. She'd imagined the sound of the heart-rate monitor flatlining (even though there hadn't been a heart-rate monitor because she had died before they could hook her up to one). She imagined herself being held in the arms of the midwife, shielded from what was unfolding.

But mostly she imagined an alternative ending in which she had been born looking like an ordinary baby, in which she didn't have this ridiculous hair, in which the midwife had noticed what was happening and had called for help.

Barb imagined her mother a lot: almost every day, in fact, and several times a day. She was an invisible totem she carried everywhere inside her heart. She had a picture of her mum that she kept hidden at the bottom of the dirty laundry pile, one slipped out of a plastic file of things that contained the sum total of her aunt's past (and therefore hers): some old family photos, a few tattered school reports, a couple of birthday cards from old school friends. If Sorcha missed the picture, she never mentioned it.

In the photo, her mother was sitting on the steps of the giant gold Buddha in Battersea Park, smoking a cigarette and scowling slightly at the camera as if it was disturbing her moment of zen.

She was wearing rolled-up denim dungarees, a pink T-shirt, and some flip-flops. Her hair was messily bunched up on her head, falling in her eyes, as gold as the Buddha behind her. Sometimes Barb looked at the crumpled photograph and thought: *This is all I have of you.* Then she would see again her mum's hair in the photograph, the way the light bounced off it forming a bright halo undimmed by the photo's twenty-year history, and she would twist a strand of her own hair around a finger and think: *No, that's not quite true.*

Her mother's name had been Orla. She had been three years younger than Sorcha, though her aunt said she may as well have been born in another time, on another planet, for all the similarities they shared.

Orla had always been trouble, Sorcha said in a practised, light way. She clearly wanted Barb to believe that she was only speaking of her sister in a light, ribbing sort of a way, in an affectionate manner. As sisters might do . . . if they were both still alive.

In fact, Orla and Sorcha – and, by extension, Barb – came from a long line of troublemakers. The McDonnells were not to be messed with. Barb's grandmother had been a fighter, a drinker and a lover – so who knew if Sorcha and Orla had the same father?

When Sorcha had been twelve and Orla nine they had come home from school one day to find their mum on the floor, an empty whisky bottle at her feet. She had died of liver cirrhosis, Sorcha said. No great loss to humanity, Sorcha said. We were better off without her, Sorcha said.

Sorcha had been self-sufficient from birth, she claimed. Had been born on to the kitchen floor and gone straight to make up a bottle of formula, she claimed. She'd had to, given how senseless her mum was most days. But, by all accounts – well, by Sorcha's account, this being the only one Barb had – Orla had found it a little harder to deal with.

Without anybody to guide her other than her older sister, she had quickly gone off the rails. As a teenager she fell in with a bad crowd and was kicked out of school. A succession of deadbeat losers came and went from her life, some into harder drugs than others.

Orla had originally wanted to terminate the pregnancy when she found out about it – not because the dad wasn't interested, but because he had died two weeks previously of a heroin overdose. But she'd had a change of heart at the last minute, a tenderness towards the tiny bundle of cells inside her that she felt she could use to propel her out of that dead-end existence.

'You gave her a purpose,' Sorcha would say, extravagantly. 'In many ways you *saved* her life!' Barb was touched by her aunt's attempt to change the narrative, but she didn't buy it when she first heard it, and she certainly didn't believe it all these years later.

Barb had been sprung on Sorcha just as she should have been living a wild, single life of fun in London – she had been just twenty-one and training as a hairdresser when Orla had died in the delivery room. To her credit, Sorcha had known what she had to do. She took the bundle home to the Warriner Estate, got on with adoption proceedings, and named her Barbara. As in St Barbara, the saint who was locked away in a tower and on whom the story of Rapunzel was said to be partly based. 'With your hair, it made sense,' explained Sorcha.

Barb had later found out that St Barbara was venerated by Catholics who were at risk of sudden death. Given the fate of her biological parents, *that* made a lot of sense too.

Barb felt curiously disassociated from this story on the rare occasion that her aunt chose to tell it. The less said about the past, the better, was her aunt's motto. But what *was* said sounded to Barb like an episode of *EastEnders* – as if it had happened to someone else entirely, which in many ways, she supposed, it had. Almost 99.9999 per cent of Barb's story was actually someone else's, a tale that had been told before she had even been born. As Sorcha always said at the end of the story: 'You, Barb, were the fresh start this family needed. The happy ending.'

So why, then, did it feel to Barb like she was always waiting for her happy beginning?

Barb tried hard not to think about the stuff that had happened before she was born. It wasn't going to bring her mother back or magic a father out of thin air. But on days like today – her birthday – it was impossible not to dwell on the finer details of her arrival on the planet, not least because her birthday was also the anniversary of her mother's death day.

The two things were so intrinsically linked that Barb wondered now if Sorcha's reluctance to acknowledge the occasion sprang from grief, rather than carelessness or self-absorption. Perhaps, deep down, Sorcha was still mourning her little sister? Maybe she had left no note today, the occasion of her niece's sixteenth birthday, because it was too painful for her to relive the events of all those years ago?

Barb had not considered this before, and as Jess's words rang in her ears – *You are nothing without your hair* – she couldn't help but wonder if it was *she* who was the careless, self-absorbed one, so caught up in her own hopes and dreams that she had failed to register her aunt might have had any herself.

Barb had easily lost Serena and Jess in the excited throng of year elevens whooping about their last exam. Nobody said goodbye to her as she walked out of the playground and through the school gates for the last time. Even the lollipop lady failed to notice her as she slipped away down the traffic-choked road towards the estate, scraping her hair back into a bun to save herself from the heat. But none of this bothered Barb.

Nothing, not the taunts of her former best friend, not the lack of card from her aunt, was going to spoil the day.

She stood at the foot of the tower she called home and smiled up at it. Even the lift being out of order failed to dim her joy. She was better off not taking it. Barb took a deep breath and steadied herself for the long climb up all the stairs to the twelfth floor – which she then mostly leapt up.

At the front door, she turned around briefly to look over at the school in the distance, at the misery she was leaving behind in favour of this outrageously good life she was about to create.

She turned the key in the lock, stepped inside, and decided there would be no more hiding behind the only gift she had ever been given. She let out a whoop of joy, and for the first time in her life, allowed herself to feel excited about what it could be.

CHAPTER 3

FIVE MONTHS AGO

Barb may have had zero friends IRL, but online, she was very, very popular. Like several-hundred-thousand-followers popular. Or at least her *hair* was popular. Barb was under no illusion that anyone followed her for anything other than her hair because there was nothing to her but her hair. Though, to be fair, there was quite a lot of it. Voluminous lengths and lengths of it. So much of it she could probably have supplied the manes for a large army of Barbie dolls.

It was actually quite hard to describe Barb's hair. Often it was called strawberry blonde, but in certain lights it would shine gold, and in others it would look almost ruby red. It didn't matter how long it grew, how rarely she went for a trim or bothered to wash it – it always fell in perfect waves around her face and gave her the look of a model in a shampoo advert, even when she was due on her period and spots had broken out around her chin. Her ends did not split, her hair rarely frizzed, and it had more volume than a Billie Eilish concert. In short, there was nothing she could do – and she had tried lots of things, including hats and two-weeks' worth of grease – to stop people from gawping at her.

Barb's earliest memories of childhood revolved around people stopping in the street to admire her hair. Sorcha never thought this was weird, even when strangers had actually picked up or touched it without asking permission – a politeness they would have extended to a small dog, but not to Barb. In fact, Sorcha seemed to take the compliments as her own.

'Your daughter has such *beautiful* hair,' people would gasp – at bus stops and coffee shops and in the queue at Sainsbury's. Barb would look up at her aunt for protection from these strangers, but instead, Sorcha would smile bashfully and thank them for their kindness. Her whole face would take on the demeanour of a middle-aged woman who had just been propositioned by Brad Pitt. She would glow with the compliment meant for Barb *all day*, and Barb had quickly cottoned on to the fact that in no other way but this could she make her aunt happy.

Occasionally, however, it went wrong: someone would comment on the difference between Sorcha's raven-black hair and Barb's strawberry-blonde mop. People would just come straight out and ask where it had come from – as if Sorcha had selected Barb at a shop. 'Sometimes I tell them that the postman was a ginger just to shut them up,' Sorcha would quip, before letting out a cackle. The fact that Barb had very little idea as to where she had come from, or what freakish combination of genetics had resulted in the cascading hair flowing down her back, did not seem like a source of amusement to her.

When they were kids, Barb and Jess had spent hours playing with her hair, adorning it with ribbons and clips and colouring it with hair crayons to give Barb unicorn hair. But as she'd got older, her hair had grown to swamp everything – in other people's eyes, at least – including, but not limited to, her personality. And then there was the evening that she'd come to think of as the one that had changed everything – the one when things had come to a head with Jess, and she had slammed the door on them. Over a decade's friendship had gone, just like that, and all because of her stupid hair.

So Barb had decided then and there that she might as well embrace it. After all, it wasn't as if she had anything else in her life.

In the intervening months, she had accidentally gone on to become one of ShowReal's most popular haircare creators: @hairwithbarb. But if Barb had thought for a moment that online popularity would gain her offline popularity, then she quickly realised she was very much mistaken; if anything, the people at school saw it as a reason to shun her, a trade-off for the clearly awesome life she had on social media. 'They're just *jealous*,' Sorcha would say, dismissively. 'And anyway, who needs them when you've got me and all your fans on social media?'

Barb wondered how lots of strangers getting overexcited about her skilled use of a hair straightener could somehow make up for the fact that all the other members of her family had died tragic, sudden deaths before she was five minutes old, but figured that for this very reason she should take validation where she could.

Sorcha was not one of those grown-ups who didn't understand social media – she was one of those grown-ups who used it as much as any teenager, if not more so. Sometimes, Barb wondered how her aunt got any actual work done, given how often she seemed to be broadcasting from the insides of Dare Hair, where she was the manager. It was funny, Barb thought, how so many people who claimed to be in charge of kids lectured them on screen time while steadfastly ignoring their own online obsessions.

But Sorcha wasn't one of these people: as far as she was concerned, the more time Barb spent online, the better.

Most teenagers would be petrified to tell their adult that

they were planning to quit school and become a full-time social media sensation. Most teenagers would prefer to tell their adult that they were pregnant, or joining a cult, or that they had acquired a drug addiction. But Barb wasn't most teenagers, and Sorcha wasn't most adults.

They were having dinner when Barb decided to announce she wanted to leave school after her GCSEs and concentrate on ShowReal full-time.

It had been a horrible day at school, and though this was nothing unusual, something about it had made up her mind.

They had started studying *Great Expectations* that term, and for some reason – probably to do with the fact that Barb was gazing vacantly into the middle distance – the English teacher had singled her out that morning.

'Barbara!' he had trilled, which had in itself made the class erupt in gales of laughter. 'Can you tell me some of the ways in which Dickens explores themes of social class in the book?'

Barb hadn't heard a word he had been saying. She sat silent, paralysed with anxiety.

'Barbara thinks that "social class" is a new app and Charles Dickens is someone on OnlyFans,' sniggered Serena.

That was it; the class was officially in hysterics. The teacher spent the rest of the lesson trying to calm everyone down, and something had hardened in Barb. She was done with these snobs – they *were* jealous – and if they thought she was a vapid bimbo with nothing more to her than social media followers, then she was going to show them.

At home that night the TV screen flickered with people whisking butter and sugar in pastel-coloured food mixers that Sorcha was determined one day to have in her kitchen, even if the closest she ever came to baked goods was watching contestants make them in a tent on television.

'I've decided I want to leave school in the summer,' Barb announced suddenly, in between tasteless forkfuls of baked sweet potato and cottage cheese, a recipe that Sorcha had gleaned from some health influencer on Instagram.

Barb would rather have had an *actual* baked potato covered in *actual* cheese, but she didn't make the rules, and eating it at least stopped Sorcha from wittering on about beta-carotenes.

Sorcha didn't respond. It wasn't that she hadn't heard Barb – she was sitting right next to her, after all – more that she had tuned her out entirely so she could apply the necessary focus to the digital world in her iPhone.

Barb cleared her throat and did something daring. She picked up the remote and *switched off the television*. Sorcha looked up from her phone in confusion. She hadn't actually been concentrating on the bake-off, but it was important it was there, a sort of background to her scrolling, and the sudden absence of it caused an unpleasant response in her, as if Barb had just poured a bucket of ice on her head or smashed her plate of food in her face.

'What?' Sorcha snapped. 'Why did you do that?'

Barb's heart thumped in her chest and her ears and every part of her body. She gulped and opened her mouth. 'Because I was trying to tell you something important. Because I was trying to tell you that I want to leave school and go full-time on ShowReal.'

For a moment that felt more like a month, all was silent. Barb suddenly felt the absence of the bake-off judges, as if they had actually been in the living room and had exited abruptly, slamming the door and dispersing a cloud of flour as they left.

'Barb!' her aunt shrieked, almost knocking her plate on to the floor in her delight. 'This is wonderful news!'

Barb beamed at this genuine expression of joy from her aunt.

It lasted approximately five seconds.

'You've done really good work so far and your growth has been brilliantly organic,' Sorcha said, putting her business hat on, 'but I think it's time we employed some proper tactics to really accelerate things!'

Barb nodded along, mentally goggling at words such as 'growth' and 'organic' and how they made it sound like she was a sweet potato herself, one that Sorcha was about to spray the social media equivalent of fertiliser on.

'This means we can really focus,' she said, gripping Barb's hand for the first time in . . . fifteen years? 'I think it's a great idea. School is holding you back and there is a whole world out there!'

Sorcha did not point out the window when she said this, but at her phone.

For all Sorcha's strangeness, she was the only person in the world who appeared to have Barb's best interests at heart. It's just that sometimes she had a funny way of showing it.

They had quickly fallen into a routine. Though the sun was blazing outside, Barb knew better than to think she could go and enjoy it – unless of course it made good content. She was a creator now, not some lazy teenager bumming around after her GCSEs, and she was not to forget it.

She just wanted to focus on . . . what was it Sorcha had said? Her brand. That was it. Sorcha may not have mentioned Barb's birthday – she still hadn't – but she couldn't stop talking about her brand and how they needed to work out exactly what it was.

'It's very important that we really *nail* it,' Sorcha intoned seriously. No, 'How was your last exam?'; no, 'How does it feel to finally be free?'; no, 'What's it like being sixteen?'

Just: 'Let's sit down and thrash out how we're going to make loads of money through that stuff on your head.'

(Sorcha didn't *actually* say that, but she might as well have.)

'Remember,' Sorcha had continued, 'you are not an influencer. You are a CREATOR! A CREE-AYY-TOR!' Apparently, it sounded more authentic. And according to Sorcha, authenticity was the number one rule everyone on social media had to live by . . .

Which was why Barb had chosen ShowReal as her platform of choice, it being the first social media app that refused to use filters and promised its users 'the beauty of your reality', as opposed to the fake fantasy presented everywhere else. It was why ShowReal had quickly risen to be the number one social media platform out there. 'Authenticity is so rare,' said absolutely everyone on social media, who had quickly flocked to ShowReal to prove just how true to themselves they were.

The problem was, however, that Barb felt about as authentic as one of Sorcha's fake Gucci handbags.

But she was going to change all that because she was going to work out who she *really* was now she had broken free from school and Jess and all the other things that had been holding her back. If those two-hundred thousand strangers had fallen for her hair, then what possibilities awaited her when she revealed her personality?

But what, exactly, was her personality? That was the question that consumed Barb as she stood at her bedroom window in the days and weeks after she left school and watched her old classmates expressing theirs freely in the grounds of the estate below.

She was meant to be watching online tutorials with titles such as: 'Master Your Brand', 'The Growth Mindset for Social Media' and 'Up Your Engagement!' But it was hard to take advice from 'creators' who only had ten followers between them and wanted £69 of your money for an in-depth course. Instead she had found herself staring forlornly out of the window.

She had told herself that this period of research and reflection was necessary if she wanted to supercharge her growth. Or at least, that's what the creator of the 'Supercharge Your Growth' mini course had told her: 'Just because you're not growing your numbers every day doesn't mean you're not growing as a person!' cheered the American woman who had produced this particular course free of charge. 'And remember, real engagement happens when you *find your authentic voice*. I'm gonna say that again for those that didn't hear me at the back! Find. Your. Authentic. Voice.'

Ironically, she said this in the voice of a Disney princess.

Barb felt as if she had watched 270,000 of these videos when, on the fourteenth day of her self-imposed incarceration, she was saved by a message from Sorcha:

'Got something to show you, can you come to the salon this arvo at 2pm PRECISELY? 💃'.

'Can't you show me when you get home?' Barb tapped back, anxious at the inconvenience of having to leave the flat, let alone in a manner that suggested dancing there in a red dress.

'NO. COME NOW WITH YOUR AUTHENTIC SELF!'

With a deep breath, Barb left the flat for the first time in two weeks.

Dare Hair was a salon wedged between a vape station and one of those 'facial aesthetics' places that Barb was sure were just a front for money laundering. Its name was somewhat ironic – nobody had come in for a daring haircut since it opened, it catering to a more sober and sensible crowd of local housewives and grannies. The salon was as much a home to Barb as the Warriner Estate, given that Sorcha had been working there since Barb was a baby. As soon as Barb had been old enough to toddle and twirl, her aunt had made sure that the staff and clients at Dare Hair regularly saw how beautiful her hair was. It didn't matter that Sorcha had nothing to do with it – the gloss of Barb's hair rubbed off on her and brought a little star power to the otherwise stale salon.

And Barb didn't mind the attention she got there. It felt safe to her, at least. She felt, if not happy, then relaxed there. She knew Caz on reception (Sorcha's greatest mate) and she knew Juan the 'senior' stylist (he was actually the only stylist, the rest of the staff coming and going as the wind took them on to better things, and to bigger salons further into town). Sorcha, Caz and Juan had been the only constant in Barb's life, and there was a security to that. She loved the sound of the hairdryers and the slightly chemical smell of the peroxide. As a little kid, she had loved sweeping the hair up on a Saturday afternoon and rolling up the fresh towels when they came out of the tumble dryer at the back. She liked pushing the buttons on the hair steamer, until Sorcha told her off. And she liked watching Juan paste the pale-purple colour on to a client's hair before wrapping it in foil strips.

What would it look like when they came off forty minutes later?

The possibility of transformation had been almost too much excitement for young Barb to bear, and it hadn't got any easier now she was sixteen and fresh out of school.

Though this was the first time Barb had left the flat for nearly two weeks, she didn't get dressed up for the occasion. It was hot but she wanted to hide, to be as inconspicuous as possible in case she ran into Jess and Serena. She stayed in a pair of leggings and a baggy T-shirt, and shoved a branded baseball cap on her head. The cap had been sent to her along with a free dry shampoo that promised an end to bad hair days – not that she ever had them but she was grateful for the disguise, and excited that *she* was starting to be sent free things, even if it was mostly tat. Then she walked the mile and a half to Dare Hair while listening to a podcast by a well-known ShowRealer about 'speaking your truth in an ever-saturated social-media market'.

It was really very boring, but she looked forward to the day when she, too, would be admired for 'speaking her truth'. That's when she'd know she'd really made it online.

As Barb neared Dare Hair she took a deep breath to steel herself for the heat of the salon. But when she approached the glass door, she experienced one of her jolts. It wasn't a nasty jolt, more of a surprise jolt. Inside, she could see Sorcha, and Caz, and Juan . . . but she could also see dozens of bright pink balloons. The place was festooned with them instead of customers. Was this some new marketing promotion Sorcha had dreamt up for social media? If so, it wasn't working – the place was practically empty. And why couldn't Barb just watch it online, instead of having to come in for real? She was wasting valuable brand development time!

Then she noticed Juan approaching to open the door for her, brandishing his phone, and that Caz had a bottle of Prosecco she was ready to open. And that Sorcha, like Caz and Juan, was wearing a neon-pink T-shirt that matched the neon-pink balloons, and that it was covered in the logo for a brand called OKHUN.com, which sold clothes beloved of *Love Island* contestants and – jolt! – Jess and Serena.

Barb stepped through the door as her brain tried to process what was in front of her. As she did so, the assembled cast began to sing 'Happy Birthday', which only added to her confusion. Caz popped the Prosecco, Juan shoved his phone in her face, and Sorcha whipped off Barb's branded baseball cap as she put her arms around her.

'SURPRISE!' they all shouted, once they got to the end of the song, by which point Barb had worked out that she was supposed to look . . . well, surprised. She smiled weakly, noticing her aunt throwing the cap out of the glare of Juan's camera.

'What's the ultimate sweet-sixteen present?' Sorcha beamed to the camera, as if she were presenting a segment on *This Morning*. She had attached herself to Barb like a limpet and would not let go, steering her to face Juan at all times. 'It's a contract with OKHUN.com!'

At this, Juan and Caz started cheering and waving branded balloons around.

'And my, oh my,' continued Sorcha, assessing Barb's leisure wear, 'we most certainly could do with it today!'

Barb had worked out what was happening: Sorcha hadn't forgotten her sixteenth birthday . . . she had just delayed it until a more commercially valuable moment.

'As if we were gonna let the small matter of your big day slip our minds!' Sorcha grinned at the camera. 'And what do you get the girl who has two-hundred thousand followers? More followers via a contract with the hottest fashion brand around, of course! Tell everyone how you're feeling, Barb!'

Barb surveyed the scene around her. As well as an insane number of branded neon-pink balloons, there were boxes and boxes wrapped in branded neon-pink paper. 'Wow,' she said, not quite believing her eyes but managing to pull herself together sufficiently to grin back at her aunt with a smile as sickly sweet as all the pink on display. 'Are these all for me?'

'Sure are, sweetheart!' Sorcha never called her 'sweetheart', unless a camera was pointed at their faces or other people were around. 'Although you might want to loan a few to your auntie, eh?'

Caz was jumping up and down with joy, spilling Prosecco all over her pink top. Juan was grinning from behind his phone, his eyes urging Barb to create some content.

Instinctively, Barb let out her ponytail and ran her fingers through her hair. She went into CREE-AYY-TOR mode. 'I just can't believe it!' She smiled widely. 'This is a dream come true. I love OKHUN.com and have done for as long as I can remember. To have a contract with them . . .' She paused, finally hearing the words that had just fallen out of her mouth. 'Wait!? What? I have a contract with OKHUN?'

'You, my love, are the new ambassador for the brand! Now, come see what you're going to be wearing!' Sorcha motioned towards the beautifully wrapped pink boxes.

Barb stepped towards them, unbelieving. Then, as Juan filmed her, she began to unbox her birthday gifts. She swatted down the thought that it wasn't actually her birthday, and how much more fun this would have been if Jess had been there to share it with her. Barb was the kind of person who unwrapped presents for a living now, and surely that should be enough to make anyone happy?

CHAPTER 4

FOUR MONTHS AGO

Barb stood in her bedroom, staring at the latest box of clothes that had been sent from OKHUN.com. A new selection arrived every week, the contents of each delivery looking a little less like the glossily marketed clothes that it advertised online than the last.

In this particular haul, there was a bright orange playsuit that looked like an oversized, cut-off Babygro. There was also a crop top described as 'leather look', a piece of information that Barb felt was surplus to requirements given that it retailed at fifteen pounds. And where would she wear the tie-dye cut-out mini dress? To the newsagent? She sighed at an electric-pink body-con dress that had looked kind of cool online; as she held it up to the light, she wondered if it was possible to be catfished by an item of clothing.

It wasn't that she was ungrateful. She didn't want to give that impression, especially not to Sorcha, who was really enjoying the regular deliveries of free clothes.

'In my eyes, anything you don't have to pay for is beautiful *beyond belief*,' her aunt had said after the first delivery as she stomped around the living room in a bright blue 'satin-look' jumpsuit that didn't actually look 'satin', but *did* look very flammable. 'Everything is filter-ready!' she had squawked, burying her head in a pile of high-shine metal masquerading as jewellery, like a pirate who had just found treasure. 'Just needs a touch of the Clarendon filter on the gram and it will be *flying off the shelves!*'

Sorcha was allowed to use Instagram, obviously, but had banned Barb from doing so because, in her words, it was for 'a more mature crowd'.

Barb was very grateful indeed for the good mood that the OKHUN.com deal had put Sorcha in. But she was just a little shocked by how . . . well, different the clothes looked IRL compared to the pictures of them online.

As soon as Barb had been allowed to have accounts on social media – the stroke of midnight on her thirteenth birthday, a moment so dizzying that it had eclipsed any excitement she had about her few presents – she had longed to be the kind of person who shopped at OKHUN.com.

She and Jess had spent hours browsing the daily arrivals on the site, picking out outfits they would never be able to wear, and striking the perfect pose for an imaginary post that would gain them millions of likes simply for standing there, looking great, with a slightly mysterious (vacant) look on their faces. OKHUN.com was known for selling 'HIGH FASHION AT LOW PRICES!' but the prices were still not low enough for Barb or Jess, not at the rate at which it stocked new items they preferred the look of.

So when Barb had found out about the deal with them that day in July, standing in her aunt's salon, she had momentarily forgotten that she had no friends, or that her only family member seemed to view her as a marketable item rather than a human being. She was sixteen years old and a fashion brand wanted *her* to wear their clothes for *free*! That was surely better than sitting around wondering what subjects you might choose for your A Levels, right?

Barb was living the dream, right there in their flat in the Warriner Estate, a regular delivery of gifted clothing arriving on her doorstep each Monday. And sure, some of it was a little . . . well, *nasty* looking, but with the arrival of each box, Barb felt that she had arrived too.

She just wished that Jess could be with her as she tore into the cardboard every week. It wasn't that she wanted to show off, more that she wanted to be able to enjoy it with someone. Being able to put #gifted on your content was one of the signs you had made it on social media . . . but doing it alone, with nobody but faceless followers to see, was starting to feel kind of hollow.

Barb sighed. The contract with OKHUN.com involved no money, just an agreement that they would send her lots of clothes and she would wear them in all her content. Which was great because it wasn't as if she had anywhere else to wear them.

The summer was nearly at an end and Barb realised that she had not gone anywhere since that trip to Dare Hair; she had done nothing except sit in the flat shooting and editing content. And, worse than that, she also realised that she was beginning to feel faintly ridiculous every time she put on a sequin cut-out mini dress at nine thirty in the morning, to make an 'Ultimate Night Out Blow Dry!' video.

As she sat in a scratchy disco dress with the blinds of her room down, trying to keep her mug of tea and digestive biscuits out of shot, she told herself she was performing a public service, giving legions of people the tips and tricks to perform the perfect blow dry without having to spend any money.

And they were very grateful for it.

'UR AMAzing!'

'SUCH AN INSPIRATION!'

'I feel FANTASTIC when I follow your advice!'

'don't kno wot id do without u!'

'wish we were friends!!!'

Each comment made her feel as if she was saving the world, not making a one-minute clip about obtaining the perfect curl. So who cared if she wasn't going to wear the dress any further than the living room? (And as the sequins scratched her skin and brought her out in hives, she realised she wouldn't *want* to wear it out anyway, even if she did have somewhere to go.) She tried to reply to each and every comment on her posts, even if it was just with a 🙏. She may not have had a conversation with anyone other than her aunt or the delivery driver for nearing a month now, but she *was* pushing up her engagement online, and with that, her followers. And who needed IRL human interaction anyway?

But it surprised Barb how quickly the excitement of the boxes had worn off, giving way to a strange, sad feeling that built inside her with every free jacket or piece of statement jewellery. The faux glamour wasn't really her style – she really did have to work out her style, she knew – but each freebie reminded her of another night out she wouldn't have with Jess: one that Serena was having instead.

Not that she looked at Jess's social any more . . . not often, anyway.

Barb shook her head and busied herself in an attempt to keep herself positive – one of the courses had told her that followers could sense negativity. As an orphaned loner, she was good at that. She made lists of content she would shoot – 'Get beach waves!' (she had never been to the beach), 'My night-time hair routine!' (in truth, she didn't have one) – and the outfits she would wear.

As Barb tried to admire the bright pink body-con dress, Sorcha suddenly burst into her room – without knocking – obviously extremely excited about something. She was bright red in the face and flapping her hands around.

'That' – Sorcha pointed at the dress – 'is the *perfect outfit* for something *very special* I have organised for you, young lady.'

Barb smiled. Or at least she attempted to – she had the sense that maybe it was more of a grimace. She watched as Sorcha made herself comfortable on her single bed.

Her aunt took a deep, rather theatrical breath. 'So, I've only gone and got you a meeting at SPARK ENTERPRISES!' Barb must have looked as blank as she felt because Sorcha rolled her eyes and launched into a spiel. 'Spark Enterprises is the number one social media management company in all of the digital world! They only represent the *premium* content creators. They *refuse* to use the word "influencer" because apparently it doesn't accurately represent the authenticity and hard work of their clients.'

Sorcha let out a little shiver of excitement as she said this. 'They are led by this amazing agent called Anna G. That's it. That's her name. I mean, she's so cool that she's set her ShowReal profile to *private*.' Sorcha shook her head in disbelief. 'Anyway, Anna G is a legend in the social media world. She's got no fewer than five of her clients on *Strictly* – *and* she insists on sending everyone on her books to a silent retreat for a week each year so they can recharge their batteries and feel fresh – it's part of the contract apparently. Also, I heard that she actually lives in one of those panoramic flats over there.' Barb's normally effortlessly cool aunt actually gaped at her as she gestured towards the window that overlooked the swish-looking block of new builds that she was so besotted with. Barb shifted nervously from foot to foot. 'And get this.' Sorcha suddenly looked terribly serious and lowered her voice. 'She. Wants. To. Meet. YOU!'

'What?' Barb felt one of her jolts approaching.

'TOMORROW!' The jolt completely overcame her. 'I've been emailing her team for what feels like a hundred years and they're always fobbing me off but *finally* I got a response. This morning. Turns out that Anna G closes the office for all of August so that she can go to Ibiza.'

'Sounds like a sensible thing to do.' Barb nodded, not really knowing what she was talking about.

'Anyway, they're back, and while your loser ex friends are starting the new school term, you're off to SPARK ENTERPRISES in Soho with me! AREN'T YOU EXCITED?'

'So excited!' parroted Barb, though she thought that

maybe she was about to have a panic attack.

'But it means we have work to do.' Sorcha patted the bed for Barb to sit down next to her. Barb did as she was told and tried to breathe steadily as her aunt looked her dead in the eyes. 'I've prepared a small speech that I want you to learn off by heart. Here.' She shoved a piece of paper in Barb's direction. 'Read it!'

Barb unfolded the sheet of A4 and squinted at her aunt's spidery handwriting. She cleared her throat and began reading. 'Hi, I'm Barb, and I feel really passionate about better hair for all.' She swallowed down the involuntary laughter that had risen in her throat. 'It's our crowning glory,' she continued as seriously as possible, 'and because of that it can be the difference between a good day and a bad day. I want everyone who follows me to know that every day can be a good hair day. Don't let your hair interrupt your flow!' She tried to make her voice brighter to match the exclamation mark.

Sorcha was nodding along looking grave, as if Barb was the prime minister delivering an address to the nation.

'I want to be able to pass on all the tips and tricks that I have learnt to as many people as possible – beautiful, accessible hair from a down-to-earth girl from south London.'

Barb exhaled all the hot air that had been building up in her lungs as she read Sorcha's speech.

She wondered why everything on social media – even

brushing your hair – had to mean something. You couldn't just go for a walk or eat breakfast or get dressed without taking a photo of it and adding a caption that explained how very important it was to go for a walk or eat breakfast or get dressed, because sometimes you didn't feel like going for a walk or eating breakfast or getting dressed. But she kept this to herself, obviously.

'Inspiring!' she said to Sorcha, who shook away the one-word compliment with apparent modesty.

'Oh it's nothing,' she replied. 'Just something that I think epitomises your brand.'

Barb nodded along. She may not have had a life to speak of, but at least she had a brand, and what, in these strange days, could be more important?

'You need to learn this speech word for word by tomorrow morning,' Sorcha said, standing up from the sagging bed. 'But when you say it, you *have* to make it sound natural, like you haven't learnt it off by heart. Get what I mean?' Barb nodded. 'And can you come up with three outfit options for us to go through tonight. We're going to Soho. SOHO! You need to look casual but cool. Oh, and also, you need to bring forward wash day because your hair needs to look *the best it has ever looked!*' Sorcha stomped out of the room.

Barb wasn't worried about her hair – she could make that look good in ten seconds – but she had concerns about the outfit. Anna G sounded even more intimidating than her aunt, and she doubted very much that she would be seen dead in OKHUN . . . A quick Google-image search showed Barb that Anna G was the kind of woman who wore high fashion sold at high prices, not low ones. But she would do her best.

Besides, it wasn't as if she had any other options.

To Barb, who had rarely left Battersea in her life, going to Soho felt like entering a parallel universe, not unlike social media itself. They got the 137 bus into town and disembarked off Oxford Circus, making the short stroll into the back streets of Soho. Almost every single person they walked past on the street appeared to be dressed for that perfect Instagram shot . . . except that they were going to work or meeting friends or shopping. In other words, they dressed like that *all the time*. Because they actually *wanted to*. The women wore chunky gold bangles and Veja trainers with floaty dresses. The men wore T-shirts, denim and Air Force 1s.

They were indistinguishable from one another, and Barb found it dizzying to see all these people instead of pixels, people who weren't in any way filtered but might as well have been. Soho was like the panoramic apartments opposite her own, or the posh park – another world within the same city.

For perhaps the first time in her life, Barb was grateful that her aunt had forced her into an outfit. What she had on was definitely appropriate for a meeting with Anna G. A uniform that actually felt kind of normal here. At home, the body-con dress with leopard-print bomber and chunky Fila trainers had seemed ridiculous to Barb, like fancy dress. On the bus, it had just felt like she was going to flash the whole of the top deck. But on the streets of Soho, next to the tattoo parlours and the production studios and the shops that only sold cupcakes – for five quid each – it almost seemed mundane.

Relief flooded her, briefly usurping the sense of embarrassment that came from wearing a dress made of material that squeezed her in like a sausage casing, her sweat providing the adhesive.

'You may feel self-conscious now,' Sorcha had said that morning as they headed out into the humid Indian summer, 'but believe me, you'll *never* look as good as this again. It will all be on the way out in a decade or so. It'll all start dropping south! You need to think of yourself as a professional footballer. Make hay while the sun shines – it's all over once you hit thirty!'

Sorcha, for her part, was wearing a leather-look jacket teamed with distressed jeans and chunky Chelsea boots. 'Keeping it simple, Barb,' she'd said, applying a bright red lipstick in the mirror. 'All the focus has to be on you!'

Barb was terrified as they made their way to the agency, but no more terrified than she had been every day walking to school. Hair-pulling, name-calling, good old-fashioned silent snubbing . . . nothing she encountered at Spark Enterprises could be any worse than the things that Jess and Serena had thrown at her. She smiled wryly at the thought of them starting sixth form while she strode through the streets of Soho for a meeting with *the* Anna G; whenever she felt a flash of panic about meeting this apparent goddess, she calmed herself with a reminder of what she was escaping.

But as they approached the address they had been given for Spark Enterprises, a look of confusion clouded over Barb's face and panic over Sorcha's. As they peered through the windows, they could see a selection of sofas and armchairs clustered in front of a slick-looking coffee bar. It was not a social media agency, but a coffee shop.

'But this is the address I was given!' Sorcha said, holding up an email that Barb could see had come from 'Kel V'.

Sorcha opened the door and Barb followed her in. A bored-looking woman sat behind the coffee bar with an iPad on her lap, chewing gum. Nobody was sitting on any of the chairs and it looked like she hadn't had a customer for hours.

'Excuse me,' said Sorcha, haughtily. Barb prepared to cringe. 'Do you know where Spark Enterprises is? We've been given this address but our contact obviously made a mistake.'

The bored-looking woman didn't look up from her iPad. 'This is Spark Enterprises,' she said sourly.

Then she looked Sorcha and Barb up and down, and with a lift of her eyebrows, she sighed. 'Do you *have* an appointment?'

'Oh!' said Sorcha, adjusting her demeanour to a more friendly tone. 'I do apologise! Yes, we have an appointment at twelve with Anna G. It was made through Kel V.'

Barb noticed that the woman with the iPad was Teo H.

'Great. Can I have your name please?' asked Teo H.

'I'm Sorcha Mc . . . I'm Sorcha M!' trilled her aunt brightly. 'And this is Barb M!'

'Full name please,' snapped Teo H.

'Oh right.' Sorcha looked embarrassed. 'Barb McDonnell. Sorcha McDonnell.'

As Teo H tapped on her iPad, Barb looked around and realised that they were actually in a stylish waiting area, with a glass door to the left of the coffee machine that opened on to an office of hip-looking people.

'Take a seat,' ordered Teo H. 'Would you like a drink while you're waiting? We have five different milk alternatives and have just introduced adaptogenic coffee, if you're after an extra boost.' Teo H sounded like she had been forced to learn this spiel off by heart, just as Barb had done the night before with her own speech.

Barb said, 'No, thank you' and went to sit down, but Sorcha could not resist the lure of a free drink, especially one that sounded as edgy as an adaptogenic coffee. 'I'll have one of those adaptowhatsit things,' she said.

'What kind of milk?' snapped Teo H.

'Um, normal milk?' Sorcha suggested tentatively.

Barb wanted the armchair she had perched on to swallow her whole.

Teo H looked as if she had just been asked for hard-core drugs. Or a gun. 'We don't do "normal" milk,' she said, using sarcastic emphasis on the 'normal'. 'You should probably know before your meeting with Anna G that Spark Enterprises do not promote dairy farming or other unsustainable business practices.'

Barb felt her face flush. She wanted to rip off her cheap OKHUN dress and replace it with a hessian sack.

Teo H continued: 'We have oat, almond, coconut, pea or cashew nut milk.'

'I'll have pea,' announced Sorcha. 'I like a pea.'

They all sat in the silence that followed this remark.

Unfortunately this also allowed the anxiety Barb was feeling to increase exponentially. It was beginning to crawl all over her, just as she had experienced constantly at school.

The coffee arrived and Sorcha winced as she began to drink it. Barb had never seen her aunt drink coffee, let alone the adaptogenic type, and by the look on her face, she doubted that she would ever be drinking it again.

Fifteen minutes after the allotted meeting start time, with Sorcha looking increasingly jittery, a woman swept through the glass door and introduced herself to Barb and Sorcha as Kel V. 'I'm Anna G's assistant,' she explained.

Barb could not believe it. If this woman with a real Gucci belt and Balenciaga trainers was an assistant, then what exactly was her boss going to look like?

Kel V motioned for the two of them to come with her. 'I see you've enjoyed one of our adaptogenic coffees.' She smiled. 'You're braver than I am!'

Barb was pretty sure that she just heard her aunt's stomach rumble.

They walked through the open-plan office, nobody bothering to look up from their screens. On the walls were shelves and shelves of awards that had been won by the agency for 'brand communication' or 'creator marketing'. A large cardboard cut-out of the ShowReal star Catrina stared at them from one corner. Next to it lay dozens of designer shopping bags addressed to various creators that had been sent via Spark Enterprises.

Barb tried not to gasp. *We're not on the Warriner Estate any more, Toto.*

And then suddenly they were being ushered into Anna G's private office.

The woman herself was seated on a swivel chair, an iPhone clamped to her ear. Anna G had straight jet-black hair, a jacket that was definitely not leather-look but actual leather, and a pair of jeans that appeared to have been sprayed on by Karl Lagerfeld personally.

Barb felt embarrassed for her aunt. It must have been like seeing a genetically modified version of herself.

She motioned for Barb and Sorcha to sit on the sofa opposite her as Kel V closed the door and sealed them to their fate.

'I don't CARE if Nike haven't been able to get their act together,' Anna G said firmly into the phone. 'My client needs to go *club*, not *coach*. And that's the last I want to hear about it.' She let out a sound of disgust, killed the call, and swivelled towards Barb and Sorcha.

A smile spread across her face. She flashed perfectly white teeth, the skin on her face barely moving as she did it.

'My goodness,' announced Anna G, standing up in one fluid motion and approaching Barb. 'Look at you. LOOK AT YOU! You are just *divine*. Stand up!' Barb did as she was told and Anna G looked at her narrowly before beginning to stroke her hair.

'I just can't believe it,' she said, holding up strands of Barb's hair to the light. 'It glitters, like something out of a bloody Disney movie. This is something else. This is next level.' She put Barb's hair down and pushed open her office door. 'JOSH!' she screamed across the office. 'COME HERE! *NOW!*'

Josh evidently knew his place in the world even if Barb was currently finding it hard to locate hers – should she continue standing or sit back down? He stood up from his desk as though tasered and scurried to the door. 'Yes, Anna?' he said, sounding like a soldier called forward by his superior.

'Look at this girl's hair! Look at it! It's like something out of a freaking *fairy tale!*'

Josh stared at Barb, transfixed, which was a little bit creepy. He was old enough to be Barb's dad.

'Oh, wow,' he said, going to touch her hair. 'Jesus. How many girls would *die* to have this hair?'

'I would die to have this hair!' exclaimed Anna. 'I'd drop dead on the bloody floor if you gave me even five minutes with a mop like this!'

Josh nodded fervently.

Anna motioned for Barb to sit down. 'What's your name, sweetheart?'

'This is Barb,' said Sorcha, clearly thrilled to be introducing her niece as her own. 'And I'm—'

'Is she your daughter?' asked Anna, looking perplexed. 'Is this glorious-looking creature *yours?*'

'Well, actually,' mumbled Sorcha, quiet for the first time in Barb's entire sixteen years, 'she's my niece.'

'My mum died when I was born,' Barb said quietly. 'Sorcha has looked after me ever since.'

'You're *joking* me!' exclaimed Anna. 'You look like this, *and* you have a tragic backstory? Fuck me, I feel like I've won the social media lottery.'

Josh sniggered.

Barb tried not to hyperventilate. Sorcha, she noticed, was looking a little . . . peaky.

'Barb, tell me about yourself,' said Anna, decisively. She snapped her fingers. 'Go.'

Barb breathed deeply and decided that now was as good a time as any to do the speech.

'So, I'm Barb, and I feel really passionate about better hair for all. It's our crowning glory, and because of that—'

Anna G stood up suddenly and sliced her hands through the air in a cutting gesture.

'Shhhh!' she said. 'SHHHH! Save me the spiel! I do not want to hear some pre-prepared speech that you think will impress me. I want to know about *You. As. A. Person!*'

Barb gulped and felt her face flush. She had no idea what to say because she was still working out who she wanted to be, outside of her hair.

Sorcha, who appeared to have turned a pale green colour, took charge. 'Well, @hairwithbarb has over two-hundred thousand followers on ShowReal, and over fifteen million likes.'

Barb noticed that her aunt was clutching her stomach as she said this.

'Do I look stupid?' Anna G snapped. 'I can see that for myself if I look at @hairwithbarb's profile. If you're going to bore me with statistics, at least bore me with her engagement. The nitty gritty.'

'The nitty gritty?' Sorcha looked like she was going to be sick.

'The *reach*,' explained Josh. 'Like, what percentage of accounts who *aren't* following you see each post? This is the kind of thing I need to know, because it means that @hairwithbarb has reach beyond her reach, if you see what I mean.'

Sorcha clearly did not see what she meant and she appeared to be sweating profusely. 'I'm so sorry,' she said. 'But could someone show me where the nearest bathroom is? I've suddenly come over a bit faint.'

'KEL!' Anna screamed out of the door. 'Show this woman to the bathroom!'

Barb watched disbelievingly as her aunt scurried out.

As soon as she was gone, Anna G slammed the door and then pointedly locked it.

'Right, now she's gone, let's get serious,' she said. 'Firstly, I don't really care what your stats currently are, only that with your hair and my talent, they are going to be off the scale in about two months' time. But first, a few things.'

Barb stared, breathless. '@hairwithbarb is not going to work. You understand? It sounds like a chat show on an obscure cable channel that has about five viewers. So we're changing that.'

Josh nodded in agreement.

Anna came closer to Barb again, right up into her face, so she could smell the woman's perfume. 'From now on,' she said, holding Barb's head between her immaculately manicured hands, 'you will be known as @letdownyourhair.'

'I love it!' squealed Josh. '@letdownyourhair! You are going to be *brilliant!*'

Barb stood there, stunned, realising that she was no longer being referred to as a person, but as a social media account.

CHAPTER 5

TWO AND A HALF MONTHS AGO

Barb was standing at the foot of the Shard, that lofty, far off place she had dreamed of for so long. She was dressed from head to toe in clothes that had been sourced for her from an ethical vintage brand she had never heard of by a faceless employee of Spark Enterprises whose name she didn't know. She was wearing an emerald-green mini dress made by Biba in the 1960s, which Anna said 'contrasted brilliantly' with her hair. On her feet were a pair of vintage Louboutins that were a size too big for her.

Not for the first time in her life, Barb felt like a child playing at being a grown-up. But she had to remind herself that she was sixteen years old with a career of her own now. And she was there for work.

Sorcha had not been happy – even before she hadn't been able to speak a full sentence without rushing to the loo – that much had been clear. It wasn't just that she had been locked out of the meeting, or that she felt Teo H had actually gone out of her way to poison her with the adaptogen-whatsit coffee. It was also the fact that Anna G had told Barb to *tear up her contract with OKHUN.com* because it was not 'good brand alignment'.

'But we have an *agreement* with them!' squirmed her aunt through waves of nausea once she had been allowed back into the room. 'They have been so kind to us!'

'Have they been kind enough to pay you any money?' shot back Anna G.

'Well no, but that's not th—'

'No money, no deal! I can put our lawyers on to them and let them know that the little agreement you have has been terminated.'

By that time Kel had been handing out new contracts to sign – which Sorcha did like a stunned deer caught in car headlights.

Barb wasn't sure that she had said more than ten words while at Spark Enterprises. She'd had millions of them whirring around in her head all right, but she was damned if she was able to actually speak them. It was everything she had ever dreamed of and yet it had a sort of nightmarish quality to it that she couldn't quite put her finger on. So she let it float away.

Barb – sorry, @letdownyourhair – had been signed by

the Anna G, and maybe the nightmarish quality to it was just her sense of insecurity. Well, she wasn't going to entertain it any longer.

It would have been, of course, too much to expect Sorcha to be happy for her niece. 'It's just the whole *way* Anna G treated you!' she'd spluttered as they made their way to the bus stop afterwards. 'As if you are nothing more than your hair!'

Barb had tried not to laugh, almost as much as her aunt had clearly tried not to see the irony.

But her aunt was too late to stop the life force that was Spark Enterprises, or more precisely, Anna G. Sorcha had unwittingly set the wheels in motion by fixing up the meeting, and now the train had well and truly left the station.

Finally, Barb was going to start that outrageously good life she kept planning to have.

Attending the launch of chart-topping Catrina's bespoke make-up brand didn't feel like work to Barb – quite the opposite, in fact. Signing with Spark Enterprises had meant a lot to her, but what she hadn't known it would mean was a ready-made group of friends. The day after the meeting at Spark, Barb had woken up to the realisation that Catrina – seventeen million followers on ShowReal Catrina – had followed her newly titled account @letdownyourhair.

'New name, same great content!' was the title of Barb's video that morning, a clip that featured her doing nothing more than swishing her hair around to Catrina's latest single, 'Killin' It'. Imagine her delight when *actual* Catrina commented.

'Feeling this, and you ARE killin it!' she wrote in a comment that itself had been liked twenty-five thousand times (at the last count).

Within hours, Barb's following had increased by several thousand, delivering her the kind of high that she imagined some people paid drug dealers good money for.

It turned out that part of signing with Spark wasn't just that you had to go on a silent retreat each year . . . it was also that you had to follow each and every one of their clients and agree to cross promote each other.

Hence ShowReal megastar Catrina following little old her.

Finally, she had friends, and really cool ones at that! It didn't matter that she'd never met Catrina or any of the other creators who had pledged allegiance to her in the heady days of the last few weeks: their messages alone were enough to fire her through life, her aunt's moodiness and all.

Since signing with Spark, Sorcha had become increasingly sullen. She had not taken to Anna G and it was fair to say that Anna G had not taken to her. And the more that Anna took control of @letdownyourhair, the more Sorcha retreated to Dare Hair like a child who had had her toys taken away from her. 'You don't need me now you've hit the big time with Spark,' she said one day, heading out to work, a rictus grin on her face. 'But just remember who's supported you all these years when you're swanning around town like Lady Muck!'

Barb had tried to get her aunt to come to Catrina's launch. She wanted to show her that she hadn't got too big for her boots and that she appreciated all she had done for her over the years. But Sorcha was having none of it. Even the lure of free champagne and a goody bag crammed full of Catrina's cruelty free, vegan lipsticks could not lure her aunt into town. 'I'm going out for a drink with Caz and Juan,' she'd snapped. 'My real friends.'

If Barb was really honest, she also wanted Sorcha there because she was scared. Really scared. She was about to meet her 'friends' for the first time and she could feel herself being crushed under the expectation of it all. The party was a big deal – not least because Barb had never actually been invited to one before. There would be photographers with proper cameras and a three-course dinner laid on for sixty of Catrina's closest friends (on ShowReal). There would be speeches and, later, dancing, while the bit that Barb could not believe the most was that there would be a car to both pick her up *and* take her home at the end of it all.

When Anna had told her this, casually, in passing, as if it were a comment about the weather, Barb had had to ask her to repeat herself. They were on a Zoom call so that Anna could run through the schedule for the evening and the events leading up to it. She had, in fact, used the word 'logistics' – Barb had tried not to look impressed.

'I said, the car will pick you up at 5:45 p.m.,' Anna enunciated slowly, clearly irritated to be wasting precious time repeating herself.

'The car?' asked Barb, imagining a big colourful van driving around town to pick up all the Spark signings and deliver them to the party, perhaps a bit like the Mystery Machine in *Scooby-Doo*.

'Yes, the car.'

'Whose car?'

'How would I know whose car is coming to pick you up? One owned by whichever cab company has been assigned to collect you! Just send your address to Kel so that everything runs smoothly.'

Barb had been embarrassed then, and she had been even more embarrassed when the text flashed on her screen informing her that her car had arrived at its pick-up point. She had clicked on the link that would show her the live location of her taxi, and let out a little gasp of horror when she realised it was parked outside The Secret Garden pub.

She had taken the stairs carefully, trying not to fall down them in the oversized heels. Now, as ever, she hoped she could hide behind her hair for the time it took her to cross the estate and reach the pub. But there was no hiding the bright green dress or the glittery shoes, or the unmistakeable sound of Serena cat-calling her mockingly.

'LOOK AT MISS LA DI DA!' she'd screamed from outside the pub, where she had been smoking a cigarette next to the unmistakeable figure of Jess. 'Think we're impressed by the fact you raided your aunt's fancy-dress box and managed to order yourself an Uber?'

Barb had looked up, feeling tears coming dangerously close to her eyes. Jess had seen her hurt expression and actually *laughed*.

Then Barb had tripped up on the kerb and fallen into the car, and the sound of their mocking laughter had followed her all the way into the city.

Barb had known Jess since she was eighteen months old. Neither of them had any memory of their initial introduction, taking place as it had at a childminder's in the bowels of the estate, where Sorcha had had no choice but to dump her niece on an almost daily basis if she was going to proceed up the greasy pole at Dare Hair. Jess's dad,

Pete, worked as a trainer at Battersea Dogs & Cats Home just around the corner.

Like Barb, Jess had no mum – or at least no mum who had any interest in seeing her. She had walked out when Jess was six months old, yet another casualty of the drugs that plagued the estate. Barb had often wondered if it was better or worse: to know your mother was dead and never coming back, or to know that she was alive and didn't want to.

Of course Jess and Barb had no idea of their similar history when they first met. They were just two children who both had an interest in hairbands, splashing water, and *In The Night Garden*.

Barb couldn't remember when it became apparent to her that Sorcha did not approve of the friendship. It was probably when they got to primary school and she became old enough and articulate enough to start asking for play dates and sleepovers. At first Sorcha said that the rigours of reception class made Barb too tired for any extra activities after school, and then she simply said it wasn't convenient. It was only when Jess's father intervened and invited Barb to theirs that Sorcha relented, but over their primary-school years, Sorcha never once returned the favour by inviting Jess to theirs.

Barb knew not to push it. Sorcha didn't like her niece mixing with people on the estate. Sorcha said that she couldn't forgive them for how sniffy they had been about troublemaker Orla, as if her dying was a relief and not a tragedy, and so Barb had never particularly wanted to hang out with them.

But Jess was different. Jess got it. And that Barb was allowed to go to Jess's at all was something of a miracle to her, one she cherished for a whole host of reasons: the welcoming presence of Jess's dad, who would tell them about the dogs at the home; the smell of fish and chips as she spooned them on to a plate; the fact that he would take them to Battersea Park and buy them ice cream.

He only ever asked Barb once about her home life. 'How's your mum?' he'd asked.

'Oh, she's not my mum,' Barb had replied with an apologetic smile, wishing she didn't have to let him know that he had made a mistake. 'She's my aunt. My mum's . . . dead.' Then Jess had grabbed her and they had headed off to the swings. Barb was sure she had seen a flicker of something cross Pete's face as they had run away, and knew it was embarrassment that ensured he never asked her any questions like that again.

Jess didn't talk about Barb's home life either. It was easier that way, because it meant she didn't have to talk about her own dysfunctional background. The two of them existed in their own world, separate entirely from the reality of all the other residents of the Warriner Estate. In that make-believe existence, they were all-powerful masters of their own universe, where parents didn't really exist and they were able to command armies of woodlice, ants and L.O.L. Surprise! dolls to do whatever they wanted.

At school, too, they rarely left each other's sides, forming an impenetrable bond that meant neither of them had ever really bothered to make any other friends. They hadn't needed them. Until they had. By which point, for Barb at least, it was too late.

By the time they were eight or nine and they had started to move away from creatures to less earthly pursuits, such as covering themselves in glitter and wearing denim, Barb's hair had become quite central to their friendship. Jess had a mousy bob that was cut regularly by her father's barber, her father lacking the imagination or skills to do anything else. And yet, far from being jealous of Barb's showstopping mop, Jess cherished it. She thought it was brilliant. She would brush it and style it and suggest different ways of braiding it. Increasingly, she saw it as a vital part of their time together. While other girls might ask their parents for plastic doll heads, Jess had Barb. Who, as luck would have it, also talked and did Donald Duck impressions and told jokes.

Jess cherished Barb's hair in a way that was different to her aunt's slavish devotion to her locks. It wasn't the hair itself that mattered to Jess – it was the opportunity it provided for the two of them to spend quality time together. For them to bond. For Jess, the time with Barb's hair provided a touchy-feely intimacy that she had never experienced, not even before her mother had walked out. And for Barb, it was the only occasion that anyone paid any proper attention to her. In those hours they spent in Jess's bedroom, it didn't matter that they were both motherless, just that they had each other.

Sitting in the back of the car now, rubbing her ankle until the pain and the humiliation of the fall had worn off, Barb thought about that bedroom. She wondered if it was the same, if there was still a dreamcatcher over the bed and if Jess still had her Chelsea FC bedspread. Or if she ever thought wistfully about Barb and their friendship.

Judging by that performance outside The Secret Garden, probably not.

As the car pulled up outside the Shard, Barb wished that Jess could see her now. That she could bear witness to all the new friends that @letdownyourhair was about to make.

As soon as Barb stepped out of the car, thanking the driver with an enthusiasm he clearly thought was weird, a woman in towering thigh-high boots bowled up to her clutching a clipboard. 'Let Down Your Hair?' she asked, ushering Barb towards the door of the highest building in London, the one that Barb and Jess had admired on the skyline for as long as she could remember.

Barb - sorry, @letdownyourhair - nodded at the woman, who motioned towards a bank of photographers. As she did so, Barb saw a picture of herself on the woman's clipboard alongside a raft of other creators. To this woman she was someone, even if that someone was only a social-media handle.

She couldn't believe it.

'If you could just have a few photos over there,' said the woman casually, directing Barb towards the red carpet and the board behind it emblazoned with the logo for Catrina's new make-up brand. Barb had a series of jolts, more than she had ever experienced in her life, all at one time.

'A few photos?' she said to the woman, incredulous. 'Me?'

'You are @letdownyourhair, right?' said the woman, looking concerned.

'I am,' Barb replied a little breathlessly, wanting to say that, actually, she was *Barb*.

'Then you need to have your photo taken. Over there. Now. Before the next person on the guest list arrives.' The woman waved her clipboard at Barb and then dragged her over to the red carpet - a *red carpet*! - where she deposited her in front of twenty men bearing cameras. Then she went over to the men, showed them her clipboard and went back to wait for her next arrival.

Barb stood there, paralysed with fear.

'LET DOWN YOUR HAIR!' shouted the men one after another. 'Over here! Swish those amazing locks for us!'

Barb could not swish anything, she was so terrified. She stood, stock still, concentrating on not tripping up again in front of what felt like the world's paparazzi.

'Gorgeous! Swish! OK, no swish then. DONE!'

Barb felt a tug on her arm. It was Anna pulling her off the red carpet. 'I can't believe I'm going to have to teach you how to pose,' she seethed. 'It's like signing a footballer and then discovering you have to explain the offside rule to them.'

Barb was too stunned to get the dig. Instead she followed Anna into a lift, and then tried not to throw up as it soared fifty-odd floors.

The doors opened on to Barb's wildest dreams. Barb and Jess's wildest dreams, to be precise. In front of her, in a building they had always dreamed of, were some of the people they had followed on social media since the moment they were allowed an account. Catrina, obviously, but also Jade, one of ShowReal's most popular fashion creators, and Marnie, who was all about self acceptance. And Barb could not believe it when she saw Pixie standing on the other side of the room clutching a glass of champagne. Pixie, the most brilliant make-up artist ever to have started a social media account!

'Close your mouth, sweetheart,' Anna said when she

noticed the awestruck look on Barb's face. 'You're not a competition winner. I can see I'm going to have to stick close to you all evening until you get used to this,' she continued, a hint of exasperation in her voice. 'Follow me and do as I say, and you can't go wrong.'

And so Barb did just that. She tottered after Anna, who turned away all offers of champagne on her behalf. 'You're a clean-cut hair creator who also happens to still be a child,' snapped Anna.

Barb realised that her new boss – her agent? Her manager? she could not get her head around it – was leading her straight to Catrina. She swallowed down the jolts, taking a deep breath and trying to will away the heat rising in her face.

'Catrina, this is @letdownyourhair,' announced Anna, by way of introduction.

Catrina, resplendent in a black PVC dress that did not appear to have come from OKHUN.com, looked blank. '*Qui?*' she said with a flourish and an ever-so-slightly haughty laugh.

'Our new signing. The hair girl,' explained Anna.

'Oh! Yes! Hi!' said Catrina, suddenly all smiles and very, very white teeth. 'Oh my GOD, how could I have not known you when you have hair like this! It's just divine to meet you – I've heard so much about you, and thank you SOOO much for coming to my little party.'

Barb smiled up at Catrina until she realised Catrina was looking over her shoulder at someone else.

'Zal!' she shouted to the person behind Barb, a striking guy with jet-black hair and piercing green eyes who Barb vaguely recognised as a model-turned-activist.

'You came! You broke your no party rule for little old me!' And Barb realised then, as she looked at the man called Zal, that her time with Catrina had come to an end.

She felt crushed. She also felt embarrassed. Was this the same person she had been having gushing conversations with on ShowReal for the last couple of weeks? Chastened, she slunk back next to Anna, who suggested that they go and touch up Barb's make-up in the ladies. 'Your lipstick is smudged,' noted Anna, steering her charge towards the bathrooms.

Once there, Anna told Barb off for not bringing any make-up for touch-ups. 'Did Kel not put that in the email? Urghhh, she can be so infuriating!' Anna poked around in her Chanel handbag for something, coming up with a brand of lipstick that Barb noticed was definitely not Catrina's vegan line (available exclusively in Superdrug). 'This will have to do,' she said, putting her hands either side of Barb's head and moving it towards her.

Barb felt something like anger flare inside her as Anna pointed the lipstick at her mouth.

'It's OK, I can do it myself,' she said.

'Clearly you can't,' replied Anna. 'Now hold still.'

For the second time that evening, Barb tried not to cry. For one thing, she didn't have any mascara on her to clean up the mess, and she certainly didn't fancy Anna poking her in the eyes with whatever she had in her incredibly expensive designer handbag – one that looked a lot more *real* than Sorcha's. For a moment, she yearned for her aunt, who at least didn't treat her like a hopeless toddler. But any other thoughts she might have had were stopped by Anna telling her not to grimace while she applied the lipstick.

Was *this* part of her wildest dreams?

As they re-entered the bar, Catrina started ringing a bell and shouting that everybody should go to their seats. Barb watched as everyone flitted seamlessly to the tables, as if this was all perfectly normal. 'You're over here,' said Anna, motioning towards the back of the room. 'And if you need me, send a WhatsApp. OK?'

Barb nodded silently.

'Right, have fun.' And then Anna disappeared to the top of the table to take her place next to Catrina.

Barb hovered by her allotted table. Everybody had a place that was marked with a personalised eye-shadow compact. Personalised with their social media handles, of course, rather than their full names. Barb found @letdownyourhair, and then noticed with a mixture of excitement and panic that she had been seated next to @Pixie. On her other side was a name that Barb recognised from her earlier encounter with Catrina – @IAmZal.

Zal was the first to arrive. Barb went to shake his hand but he didn't offer his in return. Another person drowning in their own self-importance, Barb thought. There seem to be an awful lot of them round here.

'Hi,' she said nervously instead. 'I'm Barb.'

His head swung in her direction, but she noticed his green eyes were gazing into the middle distance. 'Hi, Barb,' he said, finally holding out his hand as he held a stick with the other. 'I'm Zal and if you catch me looking over your shoulder it's not because I'm a rude social climber like everyone else in the room – it's because I'm blind.'

Barb let out a relieved laugh, and then immediately regretted it – what if he thought she was laughing at his blindness? 'Got you,' she said. 'It's good to know that not everyone here is looking for someone better to talk to.' She winced at her words. 'I didn't mean to say looking,' she said. 'I'm sorry, I didn–'

'It's OK.' Zal smiled. He sat down, and so Barb did too. 'You can use the word "looking" without me falling to bits and starting a petition to cancel you for insensitivity. You're a human, not a robot. And you're right. Not everyone is looking for someone better to talk to. Just *almost* everyone.'

He rolled his eyes skyward. 'If you don't mind me saying, you sound a bit nervous. Is everything OK?'

Barb was stunned. Was her anxiety that obvious? But her shock gave way to relief, because here was someone who actually seemed half decent and had even been polite enough to ask if she was OK.

'I'm, you know . . .' She stared at the ceiling in the hope it might give her some words. 'I'm a little out of my depth, if truth be told.'

'Nah, you're not out of your depth,' replied Zal. 'You're perfectly fine. It's this lot who can't get out of the shallow end.'

Barb laughed again. In the distance she noticed Pixie, who was chatting to Catrina animatedly and seemed in no hurry to come and sit down. She turned to Zal. 'Tell me, how well do you know the Spark Enterprises gang?'

She was sure she saw Zal roll his eyes.

'I know them as much as anyone does.' He smiled. 'Which is to say, very superficially. I don't think they even know themselves particularly well, apart from how good their engagement is at any given time.'

Zal and Barb chatted all the way through the teeny-tiny starter – a slice of tomato with vegan cheese – with Barb giving him a running commentary of Pixie's rather manic movements to and from the toilet to the bar. Barb was delighted to have met such a straightforward, straight-talking person, and the fact that he was kind of hot didn't do any harm at all.

As the mains were served, Barb heard a long exasperated sigh coming from her other side. Pixie lowered herself into her chair.

'Hi, I'm Barb,' she said politely, holding up her hand. Pixie also declined to offer hers in return, though she didn't have the excuse of not seeing her. 'Hi,' she snapped back. 'Pixie.'

She sniffed and Barb noticed a dusting of white just under nose. Setting powder? Should she tell her? She was a make-up artist, after all. She decided against it, but it didn't matter anyway as Pixie was looking right over Barb's shoulder at Zal.

'Zal!' she said. 'To what do we owe the honour? I thought that you were focusing on your creative authenticity and weren't into coming to these things any more.'

'Well, Pixie,' said Zal, nudging Barb in the side. 'Sometimes I feel I have to check it's all exactly as awful as I remember it being.'

'Oh, you are a one,' she said, sniffing again. 'Now listen, you'll like this – I've got this idea for a, like, viral challenge where I actually do some content but, get this, *without* any make-up on. To, like, show people the real me. I did one last night and, oh my God, it was so hard to do, I actually, like, cried and everything!'

Zal nodded along. Barb stayed silent.

A waiter started to put more plates down on the table, but Pixie waved hers away and instead demanded more champagne. She scrabbled in her bag for her phone and then waved it in Barb's face. 'Want to watch it?'

Barb nodded. Of course she wanted to watch Pixie's video. The clip started and Pixie's face filled the screen – free of make-up, but clearly highly filtered, so much so that there was actually a sparkle on the screen. Barb wondered how that would go down on filter-free ShowReal.

'Ignore that,' Pixie said. 'I'm going to edit it down so you can't *see* I've edited it!' She sniffed again.

Barb watched with a sense of horror as Pixie sobbed into the camera, talking about how hard it was for people to see the 'real' her.

'It's great,' said Barb when the tirade had finished, hoping Zal's lie-detection skills weren't as good as his stress-detecting ones were.

'The thing is,' Pixie continued, looking very animated, 'I need to let my followers know I'm just like them. At the moment, I don't feel very relatable.' She smoothed down her Louis Vuitton branded dress. 'Do you know what I mean?'

Zal had started talking to the person on his other side. Barb was just about to pay Pixie a compliment when she felt a tug on her ponytail. Was that going to be a thing, even *here*?

'Party's over,' said Anna, towering above her. 'You need to leave. I'm afraid something has happened to your aunt.'

Barb stood up, the jolts flooding through her. 'Is she OK?' she asked, concerned.

'Oh yes, your aunt is absolutely fine. She's down in the foyer with some friends, drunk and disorderly, calling me a stuck-up cow and all sorts of other things, apparently, and demanding—'

Anna was cut off by a shriek from the door. 'BARB MCDONNELL!' came the unmistakeable bellow of her aunt, who had somehow made it from the foyer to here, the party fifty-two floors in the sky.

Barb closed her eyes.

Zal turned his head in the direction of the commotion.

'BARB!' came more shrieking from the door. 'BARBIE BARBIE BARB! I'VE COME FOR MY FREE GOODY BAG, BARBIE BARB!'

Barb felt her skin turn the same colour as her hair. She moved as quickly as she could towards her drunken aunt, who was being held up by Caz and Juan. She turned her ankle as she went, letting out a cry of pain before falling on the floor.

'Oh for *God's sake*!' hissed Anna, shaking her head in fury.

Caz left Sorcha with Juan and went to pick Barb up. Together they hobbled away from Anna and Zal, towards the door and her aunt, and away from the fairy-tale evening that had come to a very unhappy ending.

Having finally managed to get Sorcha into the lift, Barb started stabbing at the buttons to close the elevator doors. Everybody in the restaurant stared as she desperately tried to get the lift to swallow them up – only Pixie seemed unbothered, using the commotion as an excuse to get up and go to the bathroom. Barb felt the ice-cold glare of Anna and knew she had blown it – even before Sorcha had shown up drunk and lairy.

As the doors finally shut, Barb wished once more that Jess was here, though for very different reasons than earlier. She realised she would have done anything to be able to offload to Jess then. She would have given up every single one of her followers and every last strand of her hair. She wanted a hug from her old friend, a simple cuddle and some reassurance that it was all going to be OK.

And that was before Sorcha puked right on to the elevator floor.

CHAPTER 6

It was at times like these that Barb wished she had a mum.

Actually, most of the time Barb wished she had a mum, but *particularly* at this time. A living mum. A breathing mum. A mum who could tell her everything was going to be OK and that this was all part of growing up.

A mum who would tell her she was too good for those people anyway, and it was all for the best. (She watched a lot of *Gilmore Girls*, her only model of parenting, and imagined this was what mums said to teenage daughters at 'times like these'.)

A mum who could wake her up with a cup of tea and a bowl of Weetabix and a comforting hug. A mum who could promise her that the night before was not her fault and that it didn't matter. That nothing mattered except for the two of them.

A mum who would say, 'Let's go for a walk to the Buddha,

eh? Let's stroll by the river and then get cake from the cafe by the lake. Then we can come home, get a takeaway from Stars Burgers and watch *Strictly*.' A mum who existed, rather than a mum she had to dream up while she lay in bed. A mum for times like these. Was that too much to ask?

Clearly it was. Because instead, she had Sorcha. Drunk, disorderly Sorcha, who had put her on this social media train and then gleefully gone out of her way to derail it.

Embarrassing, puking Sorcha, who right this moment was lying in her bed, unconscious, blissfully unaware of the mess she had made last night. Both literally *and* figuratively.

If the journey up fifty floors had felt too quick and made Barb's head spin, the journey down had felt as if it had taken forever. The acrid stench of alcohol and stomach acid had quickly filled the lift, as did Sorcha's complaints that she hadn't been given a goody bag. In the rush to escape, nobody had – Barb had even forgotten to take the compact emblazoned with her social-media handle, the compact that she suspected would be the only proof that she had been allowed in the same breathing space as Catrina, Pixie et al. She pictured it on the dinner table after she had rushed out of the door, along with the sad remains of her career as a creator.

As the lift travelled down, Barb had realised that it was possible to want to escape a place, and to never leave it, both at the same time. A bit like the flat, actually.

As Caz and Juan had tried to move Sorcha away from the mess she'd made on the floor, Barb had stared fixedly at the lift display screen, willing it to reach the ground floor. Forty-nine, forty-eight, forty-seven, forty-six . . . and on the numbers ticked, counting down to the terrifying moment that they would be out of the lift and having to explain and apologise for what had happened inside it.

Barb tried not to retch. She would normally have taken deep breaths, but that was only going to make everything worse. She looked down at the oversized shoes she had been loaned, and saw sick spattered on the glitter.

She would have wished for the ground to swallow her whole if it hadn't been covered in vomit.

The ping of the lift doors brought some relief. But not much. They opened with a whoosh, and there, in front of her, were three security guards. They moved forward, which made Barb move back, treading the borrowed shoes into yet more of her aunt's puke, but then they backed away, grimacing.

Juan had covered his face as if this would make everything go away, while Caz let out a groan. Sorcha, meanwhile, was in her own world, still shouting about the injustice of not getting a goody bag.

Barb bolted into the gleaming lobby of the Shard and breathed out like someone drowning coming up for air. 'I'm so so sorry,' she apologised to the security guards, who had put their hands up as if this might protect them from the contents of the lift (and Sorcha's stomach). The photographers had at least gone, presumably to capture the magic of some other event.

'If you tell me where I can get some cleaning products, I'll clean it up mys—'

'WHERE'S MY GOODY BAG, BARBIE?' came another screech from behind her.

Barb turned to see her aunt flailing towards her with sick in her hair.

Juan leapt to hold her back.

'GERROFFF ME!' Sorcha screamed, thrashing her arms around like a wounded animal.

The security guards started speaking into their walkie talkies while Caz looked blankly at Barb for help.

'Ladies and gentleman,' announced the burliest of the security guards, 'it's time to leave.'

'I'M NOT LEAVING UNTIL I GET MY FUCKING GOODY BAG!' screamed Sorcha, untangling herself from Juan's arms.

'Ma'am, we are going to escort you and your friends from the building now for breaching security,' said Mr Burly, looking absolutely furious. 'I suggest you do as we say before we are forced to call for reinforcements.'

'Reinforcements?' gasped Caz.

'The police,' Barb explained.

'I DON'T WANT THE POLICE, I WANNA GOODY BAG!' shrieked Sorcha as the security guards moved towards her in unison. They looked at each other, nodded, and then they picked her up by the wrists and ankles and carried her outside where they unceremoniously dumped her on the pavement, pointedly away from the red carpet. Then they marched back into the building and gave Barb, Caz and Juan a look that said they would be next if they didn't leave pronto.

Which was fine. It wasn't as if they wanted to *stay*.

As Barb went through the revolving doors, she saw the woman with the thigh-high boots staring at her. The woman gave her an insincere smile and then waved her clipboard at her as if to say goodbye.

Barb was going to wave back but she decided to give her the finger instead.

There was no car waiting to take Barb home, and she wouldn't have wanted one anyway. The chances were that Sorcha would have thrown up in it, and none of them had the money to pay the cleaning fees. They walked along the river to sober Sorcha up – and by walk, what that meant was hold her up and drag her past the Globe, the Tate Modern, and various hot-dog sellers who had seen it all before, until she was standing straight enough for them to get on a bus.

Caz and Juan escaped as soon as they could, waving goodbye to their boss and her niece as they clambered on to the 344. There was no way Barb was getting Sorcha up the stairs to the top deck, so they sat at the bottom, Sorcha collapsing into her seat.

Barb was relieved that they weren't the most obvious passengers on the bus. Behind them was a man, about Sorcha's age, shouting down the phone while his daughter – or the person she presumed to be his daughter – sat silent beside him. Barb felt a pang for the girl, who she guessed was a couple of years younger than her, and wondered what her story was.

Just for a moment, she didn't feel so alone.

Sorcha let out a groan before passing out, slumped on Barb's lap. Barb's brain decided to remind her what had just happened. 'Please don't let anyone have filmed it,' she prayed, as she started scrolling through her phone. If they had, they weren't posting about it – instead, their feeds were filled with glamorous pictures of place settings and pouting selfies with Catrina and other influencers. Barb was grateful for the vanity of everyone there, not to mention Anna G. She guessed that there was no way her manager was going to let Sorcha's little outburst overshadow Catrina's big launch. But she also felt a pang of regret that she wasn't in the pictures, glittering and glamorous for all the world to see.

And was Anna G even still her manager? Barb thought about sending her a message to apologise, but she decided against it. She imagined she was the last person Anna wanted to hear from right then.

Instead, she grabbed an old copy of the *Metro* that had been left on the seat and bent down awkwardly, over and around her aunt's head in her lap, to use the paper to try to wipe some of the sick off the Louboutins. She grimaced, wondering how she could hand them back in such a state. They were a mess. As was she. She silently prayed that Jess and Serena wouldn't see them when they got off the bus.

Defeated, she straightened up, then felt a pat on her back. For a moment she wondered if Sorcha had woken up but it had come from the seat behind. She turned around to see the girl, her father still shouting into his phone. The girl was shaking in her seat, her face glowing.

'I follow you,' she said as Barb tried to hide the sick-stained copy of the *Metro* under her feet. 'I love your posts, and your hair and all that. But, you know, it's nice to see that you're not so different to the rest of us.' She motioned towards the slumped body of Sorcha. 'It makes me feel a bit better, knowing that even with all those followers and that beautiful hair, you're still just trying to do your best. It's nice.' The girl nodded sweetly.

Barb nodded back.

'Thanks,' she said, tears pricking her eyes. 'That means more than you could know.'

Thankfully Jess and Serena were nowhere to be seen when they got back to the Warriner Estate. Barb had to haul her aunt up every single one of the steps to the twelfth floor, huffing and puffing and hoping nobody would notice – not that any of the residents would bother to help even if they did. The lift still wasn't working – of course – but she'd had enough of lifts for one night.

Barb took off her shoes as soon as she got through the door – she was desperate to strip off the night. But first she had to deal with Sorcha, who was still only half conscious. She put her to bed in the recovery position – one of the only useful facts she had picked up at school during a first-aid lesson – fully clothed.

Then she went into the bathroom and scrubbed off her make-up, before hanging up the dress in the cupboard, next to all the OKHUN ones. She dreaded what Anna G was going to say when she saw the state that it, and the shoes, were in.

Don't think about that right now, said Barb to herself, as she got ready for bed. *Don't think about it.* As she climbed into bed, it gave an ominous sway beneath her and then toppled to one side.

Her bed had collapsed.

Of course it had. Of course it *bloody* had.

Barb had slept on the sofa under a throw, waking at 5 a.m. as the light started streaming through the windows. She imagined this was what a hangover felt like, but she couldn't be sure. *Perhaps I could ask Sorcha*, Barb thought wryly to herself, before chastising herself for being so cruel.

Through the open door of her aunt's bedroom she could hear the thundering snores that told her Sorcha was very much alive, if not exactly well. Relieved that nothing terrible had happened to her in the night – or nothing *more* terrible than throwing up in the lift of the Shard – Barb did what she did every morning before she got up, before she went to the loo or looked in the mirror or had breakfast or took a breath: she checked her phone.

To her horror, her screen looked like the end of a movie, except with notifications instead of credits. For a terrible moment, Barb wondered if someone *had* captured the events of last night and posted them online, which would well and truly be the end of it.

But it wasn't Barb and Sorcha who were the source of these notifications: it was Pixie. Barb scrolled through the messages, trying to piece together what had happened.

'INFLUENCER LOSES IT ONLINE' screamed one notification.

'WATCH AS PIXIE POURS SCORN OVER SHOWREAL PALS!' wailed another.

In the four hours between Pixie taking to the airwaves and Barb waking up, someone had managed to delete her Live so Barb couldn't find the source. But the damage had already been done: every moment had been screen-grabbed and captured so that the rest of the world could wake up and – presumably – savour Pixie's downfall.

'THIS IS WHAT I AM REDUCED TO!' she had apparently shouted at her two million followers, the screen grab of the video showing mascara streaks down her face.

'I am basically a DRUG ADDICT because of this horrible, fake, back-stabbing world I work in!' she shrieked in a now viral video.

Barb felt a twisting in her stomach. The white substance under her nose hadn't been setting powder, but cocaine. The real Pixie was out.

She continued watching Pixie ranting about how shallow everyone was, unable to look away. In particular, Pixie directed her vitriol at her so-called friend Catrina, who had seated her at the back of the party 'next to some nobody'. Barb felt shame rush through her body. 'I have always supported Catrina. We started out together. But last night she could barely even bother to look at me, even though

I'M HER MAKE-UP ARTIST and it was the launch of a make-up brand I BASICALLY DID FOR HER. Well do you know what, Catrina? You can make up some new friends, cos I'M OUT!'

Well, this did make Sorcha's little moment seem kind of inconsequential.

'Thank you, Pixie,' Barb whispered to herself, 'for taking the heat off me and my mad aunt.' And then Barb shuddered. Maybe Anna G was rubbing off on her? She was appalled by how selfish her response had been. Standing up, she breathed out a large sigh. She put her phone down and made her way to the bathroom where she splashed cold water on her face.

'Barrrrrrb?' A strangulated groan came from Sorcha's room. 'Barrrrrrrrrrrrrrb?' It sounded exactly as miserable as Barb imagined Sorcha must be feeling. Going back into her room, she put on her dressing gown, dropped her phone in her pocket and made her way through to her aunt's room where she found Sorcha sitting up in bed, rubbing her head and generally looking very sorry for herself. Barb readied herself for demands for tea and toast, but none came.

'I'm so sorry, Barb.' Sorcha's face softened at the sight of Barb and then to her amazement she began to cry. 'I'm so sorry that I messed it up for you. I just want the best for you and I saw how that woman was taking control of you and I thought I was losing you.' She let out a heaving sob. 'I thought you were going to leave me and I behaved badly because of it and now of course you *are* going to leave, aren't you?'

Sorcha picked up one of her pillows and wailed into it.

Barb stood in the doorway, completely stunned. She hadn't seen her aunt be this loving – if that's what it was and not just a hangover – since . . . well, since ever. She moved towards the bed and sat down next to the sobbing heap in it.

When Sorcha moved her pillow away, Barb saw it was covered in mascara and eyeshadow, a bit like her aunt's face.

'Shhh, shhhh, it's OK.' She patted her aunt's shoulder, hating herself for giving in so easily to Sorcha's tears. 'It's really OK. You don't need to worry, you haven't ruined anything.'

Barb wondered if she might cry too. Sixteen years she'd lived here with her aunt with not a shred of emotion shared, and now it was coming out in floods.

Barb hated to see Sorcha so upset, but there was a bit of her that also . . . quite liked it. In that moment she felt genuinely close to her aunt. So close she decided to do something radical. She was going to hug Sorcha, actually embrace her in her arms, and show her that she cared.

But just as she started to move closer, her phone began to ring.

Barb jolted back and reached into the pocket of her

pyjama bottoms. She looked at the screen of her phone. It was 6:14 a.m. and Anna G was calling.

Barb took a deep breath and moved towards the door. She gave her aunt a comforting smile, mouthed, 'I'm sorry,' at her, and then slipped into the kitchen.

With her heart hammering in her chest, she accepted the call – better that than miss it and piss off her agent.

'Hello-lo?' she stuttered, the jolts coursing through her.

'Thank *fuck* you picked up,' said Anna, by way of greeting.

'I'm so sorry abou–'

'Blah, blah, blah, yada, yada, yada,' droned Anna, sounding bored. 'I'm sure you're sorry – who wouldn't be? I'd be damn sorry to be related to a liability like your aunt. But there's no time for that. I'm sure you've seen the news about Pixie. Poor Pixie. She's having a little . . .' Anna went uncharacteristically quiet for a moment. 'Well, a little bit of trouble. Nothing that a week or so at a silent retreat won't sort out! It's a reminder, Barb, of how important self-care is. SELF. CARE!' She had raised her voice. 'If we don't do self-care, we get into trouble, as we have seen with poor Pixie. My heart just breaks for her, you know? It really is very sad, but thankfully we've got some of the best people in the business on it and they're looking after her. But anyway, I digress. The reason I'm calling is because I have had an idea. And it is this. I think you should move in with Catrina.'

Barb stared out of the window at a broken-down bike on a balcony across the way. It occurred to her, very suddenly, that it had been there for as long as she could remember.

'Barb?' she heard Anna say. 'LET DOWN YOUR HAIR? ARE YOU THERE?'

Barb snapped back into the here and now. 'Yes, sorry. I think you just muted yourself by mistake. Could you say that again?'

Anna sighed deeply. 'I think you should move in with Catrina. Pixie has had to move out – as I am sure you will understand – which means there's a spare room in the Real Residence. And I think *you* should take it.'

Barb stilled. She had heard about the Real Residence – or Real Res as it was usually referred to. Anyone with even a passing interest in social media had. It was one of the impossibly glamorous houses where you got to live when you were considered hot property on social media . . . hot property *in* hot property, so to speak. Once upon a time, she and Jess had even imagined living in one together in somewhere far-flung like California, probably. They would be the British sensations who had made it that side of the Atlantic, adored by all the other creators who they would party with in West Hollywood.

And now she was actually being asked to live in one?

Barb stared into the distance at the bike. Then she looked at her aunt, who had shuffled into the kitchen, having stopped crying suspiciously quickly, and was now scrolling through her phone as if nothing had happened and everything was tickety-boo.

'Barb?' said an impatient-sounding Anna G. 'Did you hear what I just said? You, Real Res, impossibly glamorous life that most kids your age would dream of?'

'Yeah, I heard you, Anna. I was just trying to take it all in.' Her aunt's antennae picked up on this and she glared at Barb.

Barb's eyes darted to the vomit-splattered glitter shoes.

'I'd love that. I'd absolutely love it.' And then she put the call on loudspeaker.

'Fantastic!' Anna G blared out. 'The Real Res, um, *residents* will be thrilled you're moving in! And what a relief it will be for you to get away from that drunk old aunt of yours! This is fantastic! Can you move in tomorrow?'

Barb watched as Sorcha's face turned beetroot with rage. 'Yes,' she said. 'I can move in tomorrow.'

CHAPTER 7

ONE MONTH AGO

Barb had ended up moving out that day.

For most people, moving out meant removal vans, boxes and lots of heavy lifting. But Barb felt more like a character from a children's book, running away with all her worldly belongings inside a red-chequered handkerchief tied to a stick – all her worldly belongings being: her selection of hair products, a ringlight, her toothbrush, the clothes she was wearing, the picture of her dead mum sitting next to the Buddha.

It would be fair to say that Sorcha had taken the news badly. Really badly. Barb had banked on that when she had made the split-second decision to move into the Real Res. She said yes mostly because she couldn't turn down the opportunity of a lifetime, but there was also a part of her that wanted her aunt to miss her – to beg her to stay and tell her how much she loved her. But Barb was going to have to remain disappointed for a little bit longer. She should have learnt by now that affection and emotion was *not* how her aunt rolled.

Unless, of course, it could be used as a tool of manipulation.

By the time Barb had ended the call with Anna G, Sorcha was irate. 'You ungrateful little . . .' She managed to stop herself from saying any more. 'After all I've done for you. After everything I've sacrificed . . . you jump and run the minute some spoilt cow in a Gucci belt offers you the keys to *The X Factor* house.'

Barb didn't want to tell Sorcha that her cultural references were about a decade out of date. Instead, she stayed silent. It was the only way she'd get out of the Warriner Estate with even a shred of self-esteem left.

'The money I spent on doing your room up! Money I could have spent on all manner of things! And the moment I show my vulnerability, my *weakness*, you up and leave for something better, something less *raw* and ugly! But if you don't want the *real* me, the woman who fails and screws up and does things that she regrets, because – *guess what? I'm a human* – then maybe I should be the one walking away from *you*!'

Barb stayed silent. She wondered how her aunt managed to sound like an Instagram caption even when she was speaking.

'What's *for* you won't go *by* you!' continued Sorcha. 'That's what that Marnie always says on ShowReal. Everyone needs radical self-love. You must remove anything from your life that doesn't love you back! Well, guess what, Barb? It's time to remove YOU! Go on!' She waved her hands in the air as if she was shooing away a pigeon. 'Off you trot! See if I care!'

Barb slunk off to her bedroom and messaged Anna G to tell her that she could move in today if that worked? It did, Anna messaged back within seconds. A car would be there in half an hour. Barb brushed her teeth and her hair, then put on the least flammable OKHUN outfit she could find. She gathered up her belongings and walked past her furious aunt and towards the front door.

Sorcha pointedly refused to look up from her phone.

'It won't be forever,' Barb said, weakly. 'It's just for a little while, until I've really grown my audience. I thought you'd be happy for me. This is what you wanted. What *we* wanted.'

But from the look on Sorcha's face, Barb's happiness was the very least of her aunt's priorities.

As the taxi took Barb over London Bridge, the enormity of what she was about to do finally hit her. She was right in the midst of the city, surrounded by St Paul's, the Shard and Tower Bridge. People were everywhere: cycling, walking with purpose towards offices, standing on corners chatting. She watched tourists take care-free photos of London Bridge without immediately checking to see if the light was right.

All around her were people living their lives, doing their thing – and it thrilled Barb. Is this what her life would be like once she moved into the Real Res? Would she hang out around London with her new friends, see interesting things and meet interesting people, all while shooting content *for fun*? The thought of it made her so giddy that, for a moment, she almost forgot her nerves.

She gazed out of the car window, and watched as city buildings gave way to sky, and the offices became streets and parks, until eventually they were driving up a road towards the most northern part of London where the pavements were wide and the houses were huge and gated. They had names like 'Park Lodge' and 'Hawthorn Cottage', even though they were four times the size of any cottage that Barb could imagine – or even any house. You didn't get places like this around the Warriner Estate, not even near the lofty penthouse suites overlooking the Thames. This was another level of wealth, one where walls were dotted with statues of lions, and the buildings were made of material hardier than breeze block. Barb looked over at the driver's sat nav, and saw that they were only minutes away from arriving at the Real Res. Was it possible it could be like one of these grand mansions?

She had imagined something flash, sure. But nothing could have prepared Barb for the sheer luxury of what she encountered when the car pulled up to a black steel double gate. A jolt shot through her as the driver pressed the button and waited. The huge gates swung open to reveal a gravel driveway that wrapped around a fountain that Barb could imagine being the perfect splash pool in a heatwave. She immediately dismissed the thought as childish. As the car crunched on the gravel up to the large porticoed entrance, she had a feeling that this was a house that required her to be on her best, most grown-up behaviour at all times.

Barb tried not to gawp but it was almost impossible, especially when the front door opened and a fresh-faced Catrina appeared looking nothing like someone who had hosted a party for sixty the night before. She wore head-to-toe athleisurewear that made her look as if she had just walked out of a gym – one that also happened to house a hair salon and a spa. Jade, ShowReal's premiere fashion creator, trailed behind her, smiling widely and brandishing a camera. As the car came to a halt, Catrina went to open the door for Barb.

'Welcome to our new housemate!' She beamed, looking genuinely thrilled by Barb's presence. 'Everyone, say hello to the magical, glorious @letdownyourhair!!' Catrina presented to Jade's camera as if she were hosting a morning magazine show. *Very Sorcha*, Barb observed. But the vibe didn't seem so weird here at the Real Res, where between them the housemates had more online viewers than most prime-time television shows combined.

Barb tentatively stepped out of the car, willing the jolts to disappear. 'Hi!' she said as brightly as she could, relieved that she had chosen a relatively inoffensive dungaree-and-T-shirt combo from her OKHUN wardrobe.

'@letdownyourhair, how are you feeling?' Catrina wrapped her arms around Barb and hugged her tight. Barb realised she had not been hugged for so long.

'I'm . . . I'm so excited!' Barb smiled.

Catrina let go of her and spun her round to face Jade's phone. 'So if anyone watching is wondering what's going on, let me explain.' Catrina kept an arm slung around Barb's shoulder. 'As many of you know, our beloved Pixie has had to take some time off to reset. We are so grateful that our wonderful friend has been able to go to one of Marnie's favourite retreats so she can get well again. Pixie being Pixie, she wanted to be able to lift up another creator while she took time off, and she suggested that one of her favourite up-and-coming ShowReal stars move into her room while she's away. Luckily for us, @letdownyourhair took Pixie up on her generous offer, and now we've got a new housemate to create content with!'

Barb basked in the warmth glowing from Catrina.

Then she heard the unmistakable tones of Anna G yelling 'CUT!' and felt her new friend's arm drop from her shoulders.

They had spent nearly an hour shooting Barb's arrival at the Real Res, and only stopped because the light was changing which would ruin the final edit's continuity. Or something. In between takes Jade had been on hand to 'mattify' her skin with make-up that was definitely not from Catrina's new range. She was grateful nobody had interfered with her hair. That, at least, she knew how to do.

She had been given a tour of the house six times to ensure they shot it from different angles. Barb's amazement at what lay before her was so overwhelming that she hadn't had to fake her reaction in any of the takes. She doubted she would ever be able to take it all in. The entrance hall was a vast marble creation with a winding staircase sweeping up to the second floor. In the middle of it hung a chandelier of orbs like something out of an art gallery. Everything was chic and streamlined, with endless cream walls that made the perfect video backdrop.

On one side of the hall was the living room, full of gorgeous brightly coloured sofas from Loaf, coffee tables covered in Boy Smells candles and the kind of books that were not there to be read, but to look good. Off the living room was the 'snug', although this name didn't do justice to what was essentially a small cinema.

'We have a girls' night in once a week,' explained Catrina, although Barb already knew this as a follower of the Real Res ShowReal account, from which they broadcast the content that paid for the rental of this house.

'If we do, like, one brand partnership a month each, we cover the rent,' said Jade nonchalantly in between takes. 'A three-minute video for a popcorn brand actually got us a hundred thousand pounds, which is more like two months' rent.'

Barb knew exactly the video she was talking about. They had all been chilling together in this very snug, looking extra happy while talking about the importance of a girls' night in to ground themselves.

'Fun doesn't always have to involve a night out or alcohol,' said Marnie to camera, with Catrina, Pixie and Jade nuzzling around her. 'You can have fun with glamour-free nights when the only thing you need is your best mates . . . and a bowl of popcorn, of course!'

It made Barb think of movie nights with Jess, but now she warmed in anticipation of a night in with her new friends hanging out in the snug.

The kitchen was dominated by stainless steel, and was

full of the sorts of gadgets that Sorcha lusted after from cooking shows.

'Baking makes you look *so* relatable.' Catrina shrugged once the cameras had stopped rolling. 'And the best thing is that you only have to take one bite for the camera and everyone thinks you really spend the whole time eating cake!' Barb laughed along with Catrina, even though she didn't find the idea of having one bite particularly funny.

There was a gym by the kitchen, featuring state of the art treadmills and spin bikes. And the garden . . . well, the garden was unlike anything Barb had ever imagined. It felt as big and as spacious as Battersea Park, but it had its own heated swimming pool. It was like something out of a fantasy. As Barb stood surveying the lush green and bright blues in front of her, she realised that this *was* her fantasy. Her and Jess's fantasy. And now she was living it, while back in south London, Jess was stuck at Queenstown Academy.

A surge of elation ran through her at that thought. But it didn't feel good.

Barb's new room was twice the size of the one in her flat at the Warriner Estate, but just as soulless. It had pale pink walls, deep cream carpet that her feet sank into like slippers, and a bed so big she wondered if it needed its own postcode. There was an en suite bathroom featuring not one, but two sinks – presumably so you could switch it up if you got bored. The free-standing bath alone was the size of Barb and Sorcha's bathroom back in south London, and there was a television set into one wall so that you could watch Netflix while soaking in the bath. It was all reached via a small corridor that doubled up as a walk-in wardrobe. She began to imagine what Sorcha would think, but then immediately tried to shake her aunt out of her mind. It made her feel too guilty.

'All yours,' barked Anna G once the filming was over, 'for the price of a few minutes of content a month.' Barb sat down on the bed and bounced up and down on it. Anna G stood in the doorway and rolled her eyes. 'First, some rules. You are not to post about being here for seven days. We don't want it to look like you've usurped Pixie before her bed is even cold. No drinking on camera, you're underage, though I couldn't give a toss what you do off it. Just don't get caught, OK?'

Barb nodded, feeling terrified.

'Every morning you need to be downstairs at 9 a.m. for the daily content meeting. If you miss it more than once for reasons that are not to do with you being elsewhere working, then you risk losing your place in the house. What goes on in the house, stays in the house – unless it's on camera and you're being paid for it. No pranks, we're not that kind of place. We're *classier*.' She shot Barb a look, as if this was something she needed to pay particular attention to. 'And no filming anyone without their permission. Got it?'

Barb nodded again.

'Great. Well, enjoy.' Anna G looked her up and down with a sneer. 'I'll send an assistant tomorrow with some half-decent clothes. Now try and cause less trouble than your predecessor.'

Anna G swished her hair and was gone.

Barb sat on the bed marvelling at the size of the room. *What's next?* she thought. She wondered what Catrina, Jade and Marnie were up to. She went over to her bedroom door and peered into the hall. All the other bedroom doors were shut and the only sign of life was the sound of Catrina's voice coming from her bedroom as she sang along to a song that Barb vaguely recognised as the latest hit of another ShowRealer. She couldn't hear if anyone was downstairs over the dulcet tones of Catrina's singing.

Barb crept along the hall and decided to knock on Marnie's door. Marnie was all about friendship, tolerance and acceptance, so she was the best person to approach about what happens next, Barb reasoned. She rapped lightly on the door and as she waited for a response she stared down at the marble entrance hall and imagined all the fun they were going to have, all the laughs they would capture on camera for ShowReal.

Nobody had answered the door so she rapped again.

Maybe Marnie wasn't there? Maybe she was asleep? Maybe she had her AirPods on to block out the sound of Catrina singing? Just as Barb was about to give up, the door swung open, revealing a furious-looking Marnie.

'WHAT?' she snapped and Barb almost jumped out of her own skin.

'Don't act all surprised. You're the one who knocked at my door while I was trying to bloody meditate. What do you want?'

'Oh, I'm so sorry,' burbled Barb.

'Don't apologise, it makes you look weak.'

'I'm sorr—'

'I said, DON'T APOLOGISE. Jesus.' Marnie was wearing a neon-coloured kimono that was so bright it threatened to give Barb a headache. No wonder she couldn't meditate wearing that, Barb thought.

'OK, I won't. I just . . .' Barb was suddenly lost for words.

'What? Spit it out? Use the voice you were given, LIKE OUR CATRINA OVER THERE!'

Was she training for some kind of tough-love course? Barb wondered.

'I was just wondering if you wanted to, like, hang out.' Barb forced a smile on to her face. 'Now that we're housemates and all that.'

Marnie let out a guttural sigh. Behind Barb, from down the hall, came Catrina's voice. Her speaking voice, that is.

'Don't bother with her, @letdownyourhair! Marnie's so good at laying down boundaries that it's almost *impossible* to get to know her. Why don't you come hang with me?'

Marnie slammed the door shut, and Barb turned to see Catrina smiling sweetly. 'Come on. I was only practising some notes to a song I rejected from these lame producers. It's ended up with some desperate ShowRealer who claims to write all their own music.' Catrina coughed out a laugh. 'Let's go and pretend to eat cake together!' She motioned towards the stairs. 'After all, you're supposed to be my new best friend so I'd better find out a bit more about you!'

In the snug, next to a tray of uneaten cake, Catrina hadn't actually asked Barb anything about herself, but Barb *had* learnt a lot about Catrina and how the Real Res really worked.

'Jade's barely here,' Catrina told her, chewing gum and scrolling through her phone. 'She actually lives with her boyfriend in east London but comes here when there's content to be filmed. Fashion types!' Catrina briefly looked up from her phone and narrowed her eyes at Barb. 'Marnie is so accepting of herself that she doesn't actually spend any time with anyone else. Like, anyone. She only leaves her room to go and do motivational talks or silent retreats. And you know all that bullshit she spouts about not caring what other people think? Well the only reason she says that is because everyone hates her.'

'Oh,' said Barb, trying not to sound too disappointed as the image of her hanging out with her new friend squad began to fade.

'Yeah, I'm the only one you can really trust in here, @letdownyour . . .' Catrina stopped and really took her in. 'What *is* your name, by the way?'

'It's Barb,' said Barb flatly.

'Barb.' Catrina nodded. 'Interesting. I think I'll stick with your handle if you don't mind. Anyway, let's fix something to eat and get an early night. It's been a big day for you!'

'We could just have the cake?' Barb suggested.

Catrina shook her head. 'Nuh-uh. We absolutely *cannot* just have the cake.'

Later, as Barb wolfed down a miso soup handed to her by her new best friend, she thought of Sorcha's measly dinners. Barb had come quite far by getting to the Real Res, so why did she feel like she hadn't moved at all?

That night Barb lay in bed unable to sleep. Even though Anna G appeared to have employed a team to scrub Pixie clean from the room, the ghost of her was everywhere. What had caused her to be so irate and post that rant?

Where was she now? And why did Jade and Marnie lock themselves away from Catrina when she seemed so damn sweet?

Barb scrolled through her feed, unable to contain her excitement at the prospect of posting about her place in the Real Res. Her engagement was steady but she knew it was going to go through the roof once she was announced, and she could barely contain her glee at the thought of Jess (and Serena) realising she was now an official Real Resident.

As she checked her messages, she noticed a voice note from @IAamZal. The party had only been the night before, and yet to Barb, it felt like a whole lifetime had happened in between. A genuine sense of elation ran through her as she began to listen to it play.

'Hi, Barb, it's me, Zal, from last night. Just checking in with you as you beat a rather hasty retreat. Anyway, I tend to voice note because it's a bit easier. So if you want to chat, hi! And if not, it was truly nice to meet you!'

Barb wanted to play Zal's message over and over again, but she was too scared of being overheard, even though the house was huge and she felt approximately half a mile away from the nearest bedroom. Quietly she started to compose a voice note.

'Err, hi!' She quickly deleted it, appalled by the 'Err'.

'Hi, Zal, great to hear from you. I'm sorry I left so quickly, my aunt was a bit . . .'

115

She reached for a word but was unsure of what to say next.

She went to delete it but accidentally hit send. Damn. She needed to record another note, quick.

'Sorry, not so great with voice notes. Yeah, so my aunt wasn't very well and I had to leave, but all is cool now. How was the rest of your night?'

That had to be the cringiest response ever.

Within moments she could see that he had listened to it and her heart leapt into her mouth as he recorded a response.

@IAmZal: 'Firstly, thank you for responding with a voice note! Often people respond with written messages, which is fine, because I have my screen reader which is like this device for visually impaired people that reads out messages from people who are so used to living in a sighted world that they forget not all of us can read. Anyway, it makes even the most emotional messages I receive sound completely robotic. Honestly, I swear my life is being narrated by Stephen Hawking.'

Barb laughed and went to record a response.

@letdownyourhair: 'I can talk in a robotic voice if it would make you feel more comfortable?'

@IAmZal: 'IF. YOU. COULD. TALK. LIKE. THIS. THAT. WOULD. BE. MOST. HELPFUL.'

Barb hadn't stopped laughing before another voice message appeared.

@IAmZal: 'But seriously, are you OK? It sounded like your aunt was in a bit of trouble, to put it mildly.'

@letdownyouhair: 'My aunt was just being my aunt. Anyway, it's OK. I don't have to worry too much about her now. I've actually just moved into the Real Res – with Catrina and Marnie and Jade. It's kind of cool. Not what I expected, but cool.'

She could see that Zal had listened to the message, but no response came. She stared at the screen for what seemed like ages, hoping to see the words '@IAmZal is recording', but they didn't appear. When Zal's light switched to offline, she put down her phone in disappointment. Why had he suddenly gone quiet? Had she said something to offend him? She wondered if she had sounded heartless, dismissing her aunt so quickly? Maybe she was heartless – she had moved in here very quickly. A thousand thoughts flooded her brain as she tried to get to sleep.

She lay awake in her king-size bed for most of the night, alternating between staring at the ceiling wondering what Sorcha was doing back in their flat and checking her phone for a response from Zal. None came.

She must have fallen asleep at some point because the next thing she knew she was awoken by a banging on the bedroom door accompanied by Catrina yelling, '9 A.M., @LETDOWNYOURHAIR – MORNING MEETING TIME!' from the other side of the bedroom door.

'Coming!' Barb startled.

The door swung open. Catrina stood, looking perfectly made up. 'Maybe try setting an alarm.' She smiled, not entirely convincingly. 'My voice is my most important asset and I don't appreciate having to shout.'

Before Barb could reply, the door slammed shut again.

Barb couldn't believe she was going to be late on her first morning. She stumbled down the stairs in her pyjamas to find her housemates dressed, perfectly made up and camera-ready sitting at the large kitchen table. Sitting among them was Josh, Anna G's creepy deputy, sipping on a dark green concoction and staring at an iPad.

'She graces us with her presence,' snarked Marnie.

'Morning, @letdownyourhair!' Catrina sang the greeting, ignoring Marnie. 'Can I get you something to eat?'

'Oh, that's so kind of you.' Barb smiled, relieved that Catrina clearly wasn't cross with her any more. 'Is there any Weetabix?'

Josh snorted out some of his green juice on to the table and Jade started laughing hysterically. Marnie looked thoroughly bored.

'Have I said something wrong?' Barb felt a jolt starting in her stomach.

'Weetabix?' howled Jade. 'What are you? Six?'

'Don't be a bitch,' said Catrina.

'Ooh, you can talk,' snapped Marnie.

'Excuse this lot, they've not had their coffee yet.' Catrina smiled. 'We don't have Weetabix here. We only have breakfast goods from Sun Shyne, the vegan, gluten-free brand that we have an exclusive deal with. It's the sister brand of Night Thyme, who made the delicious CBD-infused miso soup I gave you last night.'

'Oh right.' Barb nodded, acknowledging that, *of course*, this would be the case. 'Um, I'm OK. I'll just get myself some water.'

'There's specially filtered water in the fridge,' said Catrina, nodding towards a refrigerator that looked a little bit like a spaceship. Barb hoped nobody would notice her filling up her cup from the tap.

'Right, ladies, quick update on Pixie,' said Josh, looking up from his iPad. 'She has willingly booked herself into a rehab clinic in Wiltshire, although I'm not sure how long she's going to remain willing. Anna finally managed to convince her to go.'

'I thought she was on a retreat?' said Barb, sitting down next to Catrina.

'Bless you.' Catrina smiled. 'Pixie needs a lot more than a retreat.'

'She needs a complete brain transplant,' shot Jade.

'That is no way to talk about someone suffering from

a serious illness,' spat Marnie, looking daggers at Jade from across the table. 'If Pixie had to go to a hospital because she was physically ill, you wouldn't be saying things like that.'

'Why don't you do a post about it?' retorted Jade, who wouldn't even look at Marnie. 'But perhaps don't mention the bit where you actually introduced Pixie to the drugs she's now addicted to.'

'Listen, how Pixie behaves with drugs is not my responsibility. I am only responsible for my own behaviour and I will not take the blame for what has happened to my friend, OK? That would set up a cycle of co-dependency which will help nobody, least of all Pixie.'

'OK,' interrupted Josh, as if he were moderating a completely normal business meeting. 'What I'm trying to say is, Pixie is being dealt with for the time being. Keep quiet that we've already filled her room. We don't want her finding out – it will set her off again.'

Barb raised her hand.

'Yes?' Josh looked at her impatiently.

'Sorry if I'm interrupting, but I thought Pixie *wanted* me to have her room?'

'Are you for real?' Marnie was pushing something that looked like frogspawn around a bowl, though the label on the packet stated it was a chia seed breakfast pudding.

'Babes,' said Catrina, placing her hand over Barb's.

'Pixie was too out of it to want anything other than oblivion when she left here. But I know she will be so thrilled that her room has gone to someone as glorious as you. Don't worry about it. Pixie is in the right place. She needs to get well. And you need to get settled so we can help your reach go stratospheric.'

'Speaking of you' – Josh glared at Barb – 'there's an emergency clothes, make-up and hair package in the hall until Anna G gets you a contract with a reputable brand.' He almost spat the word 'reputable' out, along with more of his green juice. 'The production team are currently touching up and editing the content you shot yesterday. It will be ready to go in a week to announce your arrival in the Real Res, and we'll follow that with a partnership with KnotOut.'

Josh threw a sheet of paper at Barb, a press release announcing that she was going to become an ambassador for the brand.

Barb's heart leaped. KnotOut was *the* premier detangling hairbrush brand that was only sold in top salons and beauty stores. Sorcha would never have been able to score this partnership. The Real Res was already opening doors for her.

'Any questions?' Josh asked as he got up to leave.

Barb raised her hand. Josh nodded at her to go ahead.

'Does the KnotOut detangler brush really cost sixty

quid?' She waved the press release with its price in the air. But really, it was the least important thing she wanted to ask.

After the morning meeting, Jade had promptly left to go back to her boyfriend's and Marnie had sequestered herself back in her bedroom. Catrina – *the* Catrina – had been the only one kind enough to take Barb under her wing. Even if she did insist on calling her @letdownyourhair.

Catrina suggested a workout in the state-of-the art gym. Barb wasn't given much to exercise – or moving too far from her own bedroom – but she figured she could at least walk quickly on the treadmill if nothing else.

It was worth the effort as Barb had the opportunity to bombard Catrina with questions. As Catrina lifted a succession of tiny weights as elegantly as she might a porcelain cup at a tea party hosted by the Queen, Barb learnt the following:

- *Of course* they used a production team to prefilter all the content for ShowReal. Just because the platform didn't provide filters, didn't mean they couldn't use their own, right?
- And *of course* they didn't edit their own content if they could help it. There were better things to do

with their time, like engage with their followers and respond to messages.

- But sometimes, just sometimes, Spark Enterprises provided someone to do that, too. Because when you've got millions of followers, the messages can get a little *overwhelming*, and it's important to have regular self-care days to detach from the often strange DMs that you received.
- And speaking of strange DMs, in the Real Res they dealt with trolls this way: block, report, move on. If you're going to see the trolls as anything, then see them as a badge of honour that you're big enough to get targeted.

Barb had nodded along to this advice, keen to show she agreed with every single thing her new best friend said.

That night, after a meal that was sponsored by a popular chain of Asian takeaway food, Barb ran herself a bath and lay in it, turning into a prune and thinking about everything that she had learnt in the last twenty-four hours. She switched on Netflix just because she could, and started watching some reality TV show about estate agents selling houses not too dissimilar from this one.

I'm basically living the dream, Barb realised. Albeit a dream where everything was a little bit weird and nothing was quite as it seemed.

Barb put that thought out of her head and opened ShowReal. Her heart lifted as she saw a new voice message. Finally, Zal had replied.

@IAmZal: 'Sorry – it's taken me so long to reply! I try and shut my phone down at some point in the evening, in a very, very basic attempt at creating boundaries. Anyway, you're living in the Real Res, huh? Didn't see that one coming! I guess I'd better tell you that I very nearly became a Real Resident myself a year or so ago, when Anna G tried to get her claws into me. Not, like, in a creepy way, just a business way. But it didn't work out and, as long as you promise not to tell anyone in that house, I'm kind of glad. Anyway, that's another story for another time.'

@letdownyourhair: 'No way! Tell me now. You can't leave me hanging like that!'

And then as an afterthought:

@letdownyourhair: 'And apologies if I sound like I'm underwater, I'm in the bath.'

Why did I tell him that? Barb immediately cringed into the screen of her phone.

@IAmZal: 'We've met each other once and already you feel comfortable enough to voice note me from the bath? I'm flattered. Just please, for the love of God, never voice note me from the toilet.'

Barb felt her heart flutter at the ease of the conversation. Zal was just so darn likeable.

@letdownyourhair: 'As if I would *ever*. But you're avoiding the question. What happened with Anna G?'

@IAmZal: 'OK, well it's kind of boring really, but that place is NOT accessible for people like me. Like, it's all state of the art, right? But for someone visually impaired, it may as well be a shack.'

Realisation began to dawn on Barb as she pictured Zal in the house.

@IAmZal: 'Anna wasn't prepared to make changes. She wouldn't sort the lighting system out – people don't seem to realise this, but a good lighting system is really important when you're basically blind. But there were other little things, like putting in stair rails so I could actually hold on and get up them. And painting the shelves in the bathrooms and kitchens different bold colours so they stood out to me. She wasn't willing to do it – she said, and I quote: "It would ruin the aesthetic of the Real Res."'

Barb could imagine Anna scoffing these words out. It didn't surprise her one little bit. She pulled herself to sit more upright in the tub, swishing the water around her legs.

@IAmZal: 'Well, that was enough to show me that Spark Enterprises were not the management company for me. And actually, let me tell you something, Barb: you don't need a management company at all when you're doing the kind of stuff I am on social. I mean, that's not throwing shade. I know you do brand partnerships and stuff, and that's totally cool. I mean, that's how I started actually. I fancied myself as a male supermodel. My mum kept telling me that I'm handsome, as if that would matter at all to me. I thought, "Maybe I could swan around in Burberry on private jets." I know you're probably rolling your eyes right now.'

Barb laughed, thinking that she was doing the exact opposite of rolling her eyes. She had done a deep dive on Zal online after meeting him at Cat's launch and saw some of his early modelling – he had been good at it. But she definitely wasn't going to tell him that.

@LetDownYourHair: 'And did you? Get to swan around in Burberry, I mean.'

@IAmZal: 'I got a few modelling gigs! No private jets, sadly, though I did get to go to Paris Fashion Week this one time.'

@LetDownYourHair: 'Nice!'

@IAmZal: 'Yeah, it was for this show where all the models on the catwalk were visually impaired. I was lucky. There were a couple of high-profile jobs that created opportunities and built up my ShowReal following. I seriously thought I could be the blind Brooklyn Beckham. But the more I tried all that partnership stuff, and after my experience with Anna G and the Real Res, I realised that I needed to abandon that dream because it wasn't mine anyway. It was some fantasy cooked up on social media by the brands themselves. I needed to highlight what was going on for people like me. How the world of social media where everyone is equal – because that's what they tell us, right? – is not quite so wonderful when you have a disability that nobody considers. So anyway, that long explanation is why we're not housemates right now.'

@letdownyourhair: 'That sucks, Zal. I'm really sorry.'

Barb wished she could think of something more useful to say. But she was still processing everything that Zal had told her. She absent-mindedly mixed some of the remaining suds into the water with her fingers. Barb realised that she knew very little about accessibility for visually impaired people . . . or *anyone* disabled. How was that right?

@IAmZal: 'Don't be sorry! Look, it was really good to meet you the other night. I'm glad that the Real Res has someone who's actually *real* in it.'

@letdownyourhair: 'Are you saying the others aren't real?!'

@IAmZal: 'Oh, Pixie is real as hell right now.'

Barb snorted, relaxing down into the bath again.

@IAmZal: 'Sorry if I sound bitchy. I just didn't like how dismissive she was the other night. I really hope that Catrina, Marnie and Jade are looking after you. Anyway, I thought you handled the whole thing really well.'

@letdownyourhair: 'You clearly didn't see me stack it on to my arse.'

@IAmZal: 'Bonus of not being able to see much.'

Barb flinched at her mistake and hit her forehead with her phone.

@letdownyourhair: 'Oh God, sorry! I'm so bloody insensitive!'

@IAmZal: 'One thing you need to remember if we're going to be friends: I'm usually joking.'

They were going to be friends? At that, Barb leapt out of the bath, barely able to believe it.

Over the next couple of days, Barb and Zal struck up something that Barb *did* dare to call a friendship. It only existed online and in private, but it was enough. In real life, though, Catrina had continued to take Barb under her wing, playing her new music and promising that one day she would take @letdownyourhair into the studio with her. Barb couldn't help but be thrilled, especially when her new BFF had asked if she would do her hair ahead of a club launch she had been paid to sing at.

'I'd totally bring you' – Catrina smiled, sitting next to Barb on her bed – 'but Anna G says you're too young. Still, we've got the rest of our lives to do things like that together.' She took Barb's hand in hers and Barb felt the thrill of their friendship run through them. 'And anyway, I know that the part of the evening I'm going to enjoy the most is going to be the getting-ready-with-you bit.'

That Catrina trusted Barb with her hair felt momentous. They sat in Barb's room, Catrina's glittery dress hanging on a wardrobe door, her heels just below. 'What do you think I should do with my hair?' asked Catrina, striking a pose in front of one of the many mirrors. 'I feel like absolutely anything you suggest is going to take my look to the next level.'

Barb couldn't believe it. She stuttered as she looked for the words. 'Well, I think that the dress is the showstopper,' she said meekly. 'You don't want the hair to take away from it, or from your voice. I mean, that's what everyone is coming to see, not a big, flashy hairdo.' Catrina nodded along, as if hanging off every one of Barb's words. 'So I think I should do a simple, slicked-back Samurai bun. It will look super stylish without taking away from the songs and the rest of the look.'

'@letdownyourhair, you are a genius!' Catrina clapped her hands together, settled into Barb's dressing table chair and started scrolling through her phone.

As Barb began spritzing Catrina's hair with heat spray and sectioning off strands, she started to make small talk. 'So tell me about how you ended up on ShowReal,' Barb asked, combing through the long dark hair.

Catrina seemed annoyed and looked up from her phone. 'Sorry, just attending to some urgent messages from Anna,' she said. And then she broke back into a warm smile. 'You know what she's like.'

'That I do.' Barb nodded.

'What were you saying?' Catrina put her phone down and fixed Barb with a warm stare in the mirror.

'I was just wondering how you ended up on ShowReal,' Barb replied nervously. 'You've been asking so much about me, but I realise I don't know that much about you!'

'It's kind of boring, really.' Catrina shrugged. 'My parents knew from a very early age that I could sing. I mean, we're a musical family. My dad's a producer. I grew up just down the road from here actually.' Barb carried on combing, as if this was all very normal. 'Anyway, we could have gone the easy route, Dad hooking me up with a record company and all that, but by the time I was like, fifteen, ShowReal was everything and Dad said that it would look better if I was discovered' – she did quotes in the air with her fingers – 'on social, as it would look less like nepotism, more like I'd worked hard and come from nowhere. So I got an account and I *did* work hard, like, I don't want you to think that I had everything handed to me on a plate. I mean, I had to get like, five thousand followers before Anna G would take me on . . .' She turned around and gave Barb a doe-eyed smile. 'Anyway, here we are!'

Barb began pulling the strands into a bun and changed the subject. 'You've got lovely hair.' She smiled, finishing off the look with some discreet bobby pins.

'Actually' – Catrina grinned, admiring herself in the mirror – 'I've got a lovely hair creator friend. Whatever did I do without you?'

Then she twirled out of the room with her outfit, leaving Barb to bathe in a trail of her friendship pheromones.

Zal online and Catrina in real life were enough to distract her from checking Jess's social media. For once, she didn't feel she was living her life vicariously through her former friend's ShowReal profile. She was just living her life.

And this life was unhindered by Sorcha, who was pointedly ignoring the messages Barb had sent to let her know she was OK. Barb was fine with it: she spent the time hanging in the gym and pretending to eat cake with her new BF Catrina, and chatting online with Zal. She imagined this was what it was like to be happy.

Was her outrageously good life finally beginning?

Barb woke with a start. It took her a while to work out what the sound blaring out around her room and indeed, the whole house, was. The intercom system was repeatedly buzzing. She grabbed for her phone in the dark and looked at the time: 3:57 a.m. What on earth was going on?

Barb switched on the bedside light and crept to the door. She opened it to find that all the house lights were on.

Marnie was on the landing – a rare appearance outside her room – looking down to the hall towards the source of the noise below. The sound of the intercom system had been replaced now by the sound of Catrina shouting at . . . Pixie. Was that really her? How was she here? Wasn't she supposed to be in . . .

'YOU SENT ME TO BLOODY REHAB SO YOU COULD REPLACE ME WITH SOME NOBODY? HOW DARE YOU? I SIGNED A CONTRACT!'

'Calm down, Pixie!' Catrina was dressed head-to-toe in silk, from the turban on her head to the dressing gown wrapped around her frame. 'How did you get out of—'

Catrina's question was cut off by the entrance of Anna G. 'Looks like today's morning meeting is going to be a little earlier than usual,' she said curtly, as if this kind of scene was the most normal thing in the world. Anna was, as ever, immaculately dressed even though it was still the middle of the night.

'You are a PIECE OF WORK,' spat Pixie at Anna G. At everybody, actually.

'Pixie, calm down,' said Anna. 'Now let's get all this sorted, shall we?' Anna looked up the staircase to Barb and Marnie. 'Make yourselves decent then come downstairs.'

It was only when they were all sitting round the kitchen table, that Pixie turned on Barb. 'You may have taken my place in here,' she spat, 'but at least your auntie can see this for what it is!'

Barb felt a jolt creep up on her: *Sorcha. Sorcha had something to do with this.*

Of course she did.

'Your aunt sent me a message on ShowReal to tell me what you lot have been up to!' Pixie flashed her phone screen at everyone. 'Plotting to get rid of me and take a *child* away from her legal guardian!'

Barb winced, and not just with exhaustion.

'Pixie, approximately two hours ago I was woken up by a call from the rehab facility saying you had somehow escaped. Now you have woken up everyone else to tell them what you think of them. You could at least have the good grace to not go spouting ridiculous conspiracy theories!' Anna G snatched the phone off Pixie and put it in a drawer. The look on Pixie's face was pure hatred, but she clearly knew not to push it because she folded her arms in a huff and left her phone where Anna had put it.

'@letdownyourhair.' Catrina's eyes narrowed as she rounded on her. Barb noticed an immediate change in her new friend's tone. 'Were you aware that your aunt was doing this?'

'Of course not!' Barb could feel more jolts now. 'She hasn't spoken to me since I left – she's ignored all my messages.'

'I *knew* that getting her to move in was a liability,' Catrina

133

spat in Anna G's direction. 'I *told you* that she was bad news with that drunk aunt of hers, and you *reassured* me that you had sorted that part out. But *somehow*' – at this, Catrina's cheeks turned so red that, for one minute, Barb thought that steam would blow her turban off her head – '@letdownyourhair's mess of an aunt has managed to contact this mess of a make-up artist in rehab, no less!'

'This mess of a make-up artist is a little bit cannier than you think and managed to smuggle in a hidden phone, so STICK IT WHERE THE SUN DON'T SHINE!'

'I'll stick it where the sun don't shine when you're responsible enough not to have had your phone confiscated and locked in a drawer.' Catrina shook her head in disgust and then smoothed down her turban.

Marnie let out a series of bored sighs.

'I'm sorry,' she interrupted, 'but this really has nothing to do with me and I don't think it's fair that you are trying to involve me in your drama. So I am going back to the calm, boundaried space of my bedroom. Goodnight.'

Everybody ignored her as she left the kitchen.

'So here's what we are going to do,' announced Catrina, taking control of the situation. 'Luckily we haven't posted any content with @letdownyourhair.'

'My name is *Barb*,' she shot, surprised at her courage to do so. Perhaps it was because she could see where this was heading.

'Barb.' Catrina corrected herself, rolling the name round her mouth like it was a poisonous witchity grub. 'So we are going to pretend that the last couple of days never happened. Pixie will move back in, we will do some posts about her silent retreat, and then we will go on a girls' bonding trip somewhere nice like, I dunno, the Maldives.' Barb's body was now prickling all over with jolts as she heard herself being rewritten out of the Real Res. '@letdownyourhair can see this as a little treat where she's got to hang with some of her favourite creators and learn some of their tricks,' Catrina continued, not bothering to even glance Barb's way.

'Like a competition winner.' Anna G nodded. '*Yes!* We can pretend that @letdownyourhair got in touch and asked you to mentor her, and so you gave her a few days in the house while Pixie was resetting at the retreat!'

'Perhaps we could get her to do my hair in a collab video or something.' Catrina sounded bored now. 'She did a passable attempt at it the other night.'

Barb felt her stomach twist with humiliation as they talked about her as if she wasn't there.

'Fantastic idea!' Anna G smiled, clapping her hands together. 'God, there's a reason you have seventeen million followers, Catrina! Sound good to you, Pixie?'

'Does it mean I don't have to stay in rehab?'

'If you promise to hand in your phone in the evening, it's a deal.'

'Deal!' Pixie smiled.

'Deal!' squealed Catrina.

'Pack your bags, Barb!' Anna G clicked her fingers, finally acknowledging Barb's presence. 'I'll order you a car.'

'Look what the cat dragged in.' Sorcha stood in the doorway of their twelfth-floor flat, looking like the cat that got the cream. Barb hurried straight past her and into the living room, desperate not to be seen by anyone. She dumped her bags on the floor, containing the clothes Anna G had dressed her in – the only proof she had ever been at the Real Res. She wondered if she could post a picture of herself in them, alongside the caption: 'I went to the Real Res and all I got was this lousy gifted jumpsuit'. She went immediately to the kitchen cupboard for some Weetabix. Just four days of eating what felt like nothing but chia-seed pudding had left her ravenous.

'I told you that lot at Spark Enterprises didn't have your best interests at heart.' Sorcha stood on the other side of the kitchen counter, her mouth curled into an I-told-you-so smirk. 'Not like me.'

'I don't want to talk about it,' Barb said, pouring milk on her Weetabix.

'Well, I do, Barb. I DO! You waltzed out of here like Lady Muck and now you come back with your tail between your legs. How do you think that makes me feel?'

Barb knew better than to talk back. She wanted to tell her aunt that she'd have never got involved with Spark Enterprises had it not been for her, but she didn't have the energy in her for a fight. She'd been up since nearly 4 a.m., after all, and the intervening hours had been a blur, culminating in a tearful voice noting session with Zal as another taxi returned her to south London. She had hesitated before recording her message, but reasoned that nothing was likely to be as humiliating as being evicted from the Real Res after five measly days. The green 'online now' icon next to his name at 7 a.m. was all the permission she needed to press send.

@letdownyourhair: 'So, I think I should have seen your experience as a warning. Pixie just showed up and now I've been told my time in the Real Res is up, and that I should be grateful for the mentoring experience I got while keeping Pixie's bed warm. And now I'm on my way back to south London where I belong in my tower.'

@IAmZal: 'Wait, what? Are you OK? You sound kind of shaken up. I feel like the universe brought us together so we could take a stand against Anna G and her evil Spark Enterprises. Is there anything I can do?'

@letdownyourhair: 'Just keep being your brilliant self on ShowReal. I think I need more activism and less influencing in my life. Sorry, I mean *creating*, obvs.'

@IAmZal: 'Carry on using words like that and you'll be cancelled by the influencers. Keep it up I say!'

@letdownyourhair: 'I need to be more like you when it comes to social media.'

@IAmZal: 'No, Barb, you need to be more like you. That's how you're going to make a difference on social media.'

But Barb wasn't sure she knew who she was, only who she wasn't – and she wasn't anything like Catrina, Marnie et al., that was for sure. But was she anything like Sorcha? As her aunt stood in front of her pretending to care about her wellbeing, she couldn't help but feel she was caught between a rock and a hard place – the rock being the Real Res, and the hard place being the twelfth floor of the estate.

'I'm sorry if it caused some drama, me letting Pixie know. But I think it's better if we are all living in our truth, don't you, Barb?' Barb spooned some Weetabix into her mouth, resigned to her aunt's words. 'I think it would be better if I became your manager, don't you? I know *you*, Barb. I'm not going to turn my nose up at OKHUN, like some posh society girl. I know how to make you *relatable*, and it ain't living in a three-million-pound house with a bunch of turncoats who are about as authentic as my Gucci bag over there.'

Barb felt the tiredness sweeping over her head. She just wanted to sink into her bed – and then she remembered she didn't have one since it had collapsed last week. 'You're right, Sorcha,' Barb said, heading towards her bedroom with the intention of falling straight to sleep on the mattress on the floor. 'I'd rather *you* were my manager than Anna G. I'm not sure I fit in there.' *And I'm not sure I want anything to do with Anna any more*, Barb thought. *Everything about her was toxic.*

Barb opened her door and there, in front of her, was a huge, pink bed, taking up most of her bedroom.

'SURPRISE!' shrieked Sorcha.

Not for the first time today, Barb was stunned into silence.

'It's been gifted from Sweet Dreamz, in return for some content, of course. But we'll get to that once you've rested a bit and got over that awful Real Residence place. Sweet Dreamz, Barb!'

Well, it was one way for Sorcha to show Barb she cared.

Within days, the pair had settled back into their old routine: Sorcha leaving Post-it notes on the kitchen top with instructions for the day's content and Barb following them obediently. And another day of Barb faking her outrageously good life from the confines of her bedroom would begin. Barb had thrown herself into @letdownyourhair. She spent hours obsessing over her analytics – why had she only gained two hundred and fifty followers that day, compared to six hundred the day before? – and replying to comments. She started blocking the odd account that trolled her – she repeated Catrina's advice, even though it pained her – and replied to every positive message she received with, at the very least, a hands-together-thankful emoji. When she got bored of that emoji, she switched it up by sending the heart emoji, or if she was feeling particularly wild, a flower emoji.

She scoured content under hashtags like #hairreal or #hairstyle to make sure her videos were fresh, and that she was both up with the latest trends and ahead of them. She told herself that the deals her aunt was doing were fine, just fine, and that she didn't need to worry about the strangely toxic smell of the hair treatment she had apparently just signed a two-post deal with. The brand partnerships were a means to an end, a way for her – for them – to make a bit of cash so that she could create the kind of content that mattered. Barb still wasn't sure what that was yet – though Zal had shown her, through his journey from model to activist, that the road to authenticity wasn't always paved with good intentions. But she *was* sure that in the meantime she could spend two minutes doing nothing more than brushing her hair with the latest cheap knock-off of Tangle Teezers, and make everyone happy. (That video had got her two-hundred thousand likes and, Sorcha assured her, a sizeable sum in her bank account. Not that she had access to that bank account.)

She only looked at Jess's profile very, very occasionally, aware that it made her mood plummet about as much as realising she had been unfollowed by Catrina, Marnie and the entire staff of Spark Enterprises. She had expected it once she had received a curt message from Anna G thanking her for taking part in the 'mentoring experience', a message that also reminded her that she was contractually obliged not to post about anything she had seen in the Real Res – an obligation that would be legally enforced if need be.

But she felt safe talking about it to Zal.

Some days they spoke for hours. She felt she could tell Zal anything and realised that there had never been anyone in her life she had experienced that with. Even with Jess, there had been an unspoken agreement that they would not talk about their missing mothers – instead, they would simply pretend that mothers did not exist and all was well in the world. It was denial, Barb now realised, and it was good to talk to someone other than Sorcha about her life. Now she came to think about it, it was good to actually be *asked* about her life. Zal was the first person who had shown any genuine interest in it since . . . forever?

@IAmZal: 'So tell me if I'm being nosy, but how come you live with your aunt?'

@letdownyourhair: 'I don't think you're being nosy, I think you're asking a perfectly reasonable question. Why *am* I living with my aunt, I often ask myself. It's only because I have no choice – I've always lived with her. My mum died when she was giving birth to me, and my dad left before I was born. So that's why I live with her, and I probably shouldn't be so unkind about her given that she basically brought me up all by herself and gave up everything for me. As she likes to remind me frequently.'

@IAmZal: 'OK, two things. Firstly, I'm really sorry about your parents. Secondly, maybe she didn't give up everything. Maybe she just did what any decent human would do under the circumstances? True decency does not require pointing out your decency, if you know what I mean?'

@letdownyourhair: 'Increasingly, I *do* know what you mean.'

If initially Barb had felt the need to tiptoe around Zal's blindness, his subsequent openness meant she had lost this reservation. His blindness was not something to be ignored, she realised – it was something he wanted celebrated and acknowledged. It was a fundamental part of him that informed the way he experienced life, but it was also important to remember that it wasn't all of him.

@letdownyourhair: 'OK, so you tell me if I'm being nosy now, but what is it like to be blind?'

The pause from Zal was so long that Barb began to panic;

she was just about to start recording an apology when his reply came through.

@IAmZal: 'As you might say, not nosy, just normal! OK, so lots of people think that blindness means you can't see anything at all, and for many people that is the case. But I can see very blurry shapes or colours. The thing is, my sight can't be corrected with some glasses or a pair of contact lenses. For as long as I can remember, I've only been able to see things that are really close up to my face. My eyes are super sensitive to light and I frequently get migraines. Which sounds awful, but really the only awful thing is how inaccessible society is to blind people. Also, technology has completely *transformed* my life. Like, adults are always banging on about how terrible social media is, what pressure it puts on young people, but the truth is, it's opened my life up. It's enabled me to connect with people in a way I couldn't before. And using a camera in close up has made things so much clearer for me. Really, it wasn't much a leap for me to go from consuming content to creating it.'

His videos about life as a visually impaired person had resonated with his audience of non-disabled people who had initially come for the modelling shots, and stayed for the education. He had charisma and humour. He wasn't popular because he wore nice clothes or had good hair or great bone structure, though all these things were true –

Barb had definitely noticed. He was popular because he was *Zal*. Warm, open, Zal.

@IAmZal: 'Mate, I did a post about the World Cup of breakfast cereals this morning, and you've still not commented on it. Like, where's the Weetabix love? Did you oversleep and miss the post, as well as the most important meal of the day?'

@letdownyourhair: 'It's such an important issue that I wanted to really think about my comment before I posted it. Really make Weetabix's case, you know?'

@IAmZal: 'Sure, sure. I get it. Do you think maybe my breakfast content is not the content my followers want?'

@letdownyourhair: 'Maybe you should start doing some stuff about your hair care regime? That would really broaden out your demographic, as Anna G might say.'

@IAmZal: 'Only if the content involves you dying my hair pink. Or purple. Or blue.'

And through him, Barb was learning about all the ways that she could make her channel accessible to disabled people. She was embarrassed that it hadn't even occurred to her to use captions for deaf users, or image text descriptions for her images. Again she was hit with the sense that there was a whole other world out there, within the same one she lived in – a world that was richer and greater and far more empathetic than the one she had witnessed during her short time with Spark Enterprises. And she wanted to be a part of that world. With each voice note and each post Zal made, Barb began to see a different social media path, one that didn't involve endless brand partnerships and soul-destroying link-ups with people who called her by her social media handle instead of her name.

@letdownyourhair: 'I need to confess something to you. Before I met you, I just assumed that blind people lived limited lives. Now I see that you just have different lives.'

@IAmZal: 'I also have a confession to make: before I met you, I just assumed all orphans lived in workhouses and lived on gruel. Now I see that you actually live mostly on Weetabix.'

@letdownyourhair: 'Touché, Zal, touché.'

@IAmZal: 'Seriously, though, thank you for saying that. I would always rather people said things than be worried of offending me. Because otherwise, how do we learn about each other? How do we open the world up? But I need to tell you that some blind people *do* lead really limited lives, and that's why I do what I do. To open up the world to them. I mean, the more people I reach, the more I can get the message out about how to make everything easier for disabled people. But it's also important to me that I show

145

that being visually impaired doesn't have to mean that your life is impaired. I mean, I'm out and about *way more* than you, locked away in your tower block refusing to come out and meet me because you have too much content to make.'

@letdownyourhair: 'Hey, hermits have feelings too!'

@IAmZal: 'Maybe you could become a campaigner for hermits? A hermit activist?'

@letdownyourhair: 'I'm thinking, a video about how to talk to the hermit in your life who doesn't want to talk to you? Thank goodness for technology or us hermits would never speak to anyone.'

@IAmZal: 'You know, it's true – what you're saying about technology. When I was born, there was Braille, which is like a sensory thing that enables you to read. But there wasn't much else. Now, there's so much assistive technology, which means that I can access almost everything that you sighted lot take for granted. Adults are so sniffy about social media and phones and how they are ruining our brains, but that's such a privileged viewpoint to take. For me they have allowed me to enhance my brain. I can listen to books and in a way I can even see images now, because increasingly people are using text descriptions to explain the pictures they post. These text descriptions can be read out by software on a blind person's phone so they know what the image is. Not everybody is using this, but more and more people are, and maybe one day it will be completely normal. Which actually brings me to this idea I've had, that I want to run past you to see what you think about it. If that's OK?'

@letdownyourhair: 'I'm just touched that you want my opinion on anything!'

@IAmZal: 'Listen, you know your audience, and it's your audience that I kind of want to reach with this. To make disability campaigning more mainstream. So, what if I started a sort of viral challenge? Or a challenge that I hope will go viral? I want to get people to start using alt text and embed the description of the images they post in the image, or use captions to describe the images. I thought I could ask them to post a picture that really means something to them, that shows them with someone or something that has helped them to see things more clearly. For me it's those descriptions that my robotic screen reader reads out so I can imagine what the pictures look like, but for you it might be something different. It might be a picture of your aunt, drunk on her ass at an event, helping you to see that family is way more important than awful, stuck-up parties for social media stars. Then you'd write a caption, explaining the ways this person or thing helped you to see clearly, and say you were taking part in the challenge to get more people to use text descriptions. Then you'd use a text description at the bottom of the caption or alt text, *et voilà!*'

@letdownyourhair: 'I think it's an *amazing* idea and

I will totally take part, but there is no way I am putting a picture of my drunk aunt on her arse, mostly because – *thank goodness* – nobody actually captured any. I only wish I'd taken a picture of Catrina at 4 a.m. in a silk turban, alongside a caption that says "Behold, backstabber in her natural habitat."'

That night, Barb had sunk into her Sweet Dreamz bed thinking about Zal, and the challenge, and all sorts of possibilities that existed on social media that did not involve her blow drying her hair or putting strange chemicals on it for the sake of what she assumed was a few hundred quid (a few hundred quid she had yet to see). Was this what she wanted to do with her life? Was sitting in this flat all day editing images and videos of her hair *really* how she wanted to spend the remainder of her days?

The next morning, Barb ate her Weetabix and checked her phone, and smiled as her feed filled with people doing the #WhatICouldntSee challenge. Zal had gone live with it last night and already the hashtag had a quarter of a million posts under it. It amazed Barb how quickly things could build, how an idea he had told her about yesterday was now all across the world.

Even the usually cynical Sorcha had sent her a message telling her to take part in it. 'I usually see these things as virtue-signalling clap-trap,' she said in a WhatsApp missive, 'but this guy is the real deal and people are going *wild* for him. You could post a picture of me and write some caption about being an orphan, having the support of your aunt, blah blah. What do you think?'

Barb laughed in spite of herself. Since Zal had turned up, the whole world was beginning to make a strange kind of painful sense.

Barb spent much of the day, as usual, alone in her room, occasionally voice noting Zal, to goggle at the scale and scope of how viral he had gone. By the afternoon, no fewer than two million people had committed to using text descriptions, including, but not limited to: fifteen Grammy winners, ten Oscar winners, three Kardashians and umpteen politicians. Even the prime minister had done a post of the front door of 10 Downing Street, writing how his position had enabled him to meet amazing people who had opened up his mind.

@letdownyourhair: 'I'm pretty sure you're about ten posts away from the Queen making you a knight.'

@IAmZal: 'Babes, I ain't wasting my time with the Queen.'

Barb couldn't pinpoint why she had chosen to look at Jess's profile. She hadn't even thought to glance at it for weeks now. And yet, as she gazed out of her bedroom window over the tumble-down playground and the place they both called home, a yearning to see Jess shot through her. Perhaps it was the friendship with Zal that had awakened in her a need for company. Whatever it was, it came over her very suddenly, without warning. One minute she was happy as Larry, hanging out online with her friend Zal, with no need for anything other than his voice notes . . . and the next, she just had to look at Jess's social media. To check, perhaps, that she had moved on from her old friend, through discovering another.

As soon as she saw the picture, she knew. It had been posted six hours ago, as Zal's challenge had started its sweep across social media. It was a photo of Jess with Serena. They were hugging each other tight, smiling broadly as they sat on Jess's bed. (From the vivid blue that Barb could see, Jess still had her Chelsea FC duvet cover.) It was a look that said, 'Together we can take on the world'. It was a look that said, 'See how much better off I am without you.'

It was exactly the look that Barb had imagined herself making in a selfie with Zal.

The picture pierced a hole in her heart, but Barb knew that wasn't the worst of it. The worst of it was in the caption below: 'I'm doing @IAmZal's #WhatICouldntSee challenge, to commit to using more text captions on social media, making it a more inclusive place. So this is a picture of me at home, on my bed, smiling widely with my brilliant best friend @serenaSW11. Before this amazing girl came into my life, I didn't see what real friendship was.' Barb felt the jolts approaching. 'I thought I knew what friendship was, but I was wrong. Here's something I've not really said before: my mum left when I was only six months old. The person who was there for me all through my childhood, other than my dad – that person was like a sister to me. She got it. She knew what I had been through. With her, I felt like anything was possible. But then she betrayed me. She betrayed me and I thought I'd never get over it. Now I see she actually did me a favour. Once she had shown her true colours, I was able to see the true friends I had, the ones who valued me as a human and wanted the best for me. Thank you to @serenaSW11 for making me see the true value of friendship.'

As she stopped reading, so did Barb's world: just for a moment everything disappeared from around her – the phone, the bed, the flat, her useless hair.

Then it all came flooding back into focus, and the comments swam into view:

'You are so much better off without her'

'I am so sorry for what happened to you, but at least now you are free'

'We are all behind you'

'Best one I've seen yet . . . that girl is a 🦆 '

And finally, from Serena: 'There is more heart in this one post than in that person's entire social media feed.'

151

Barb dove under the duvet. Outside she could hear the estate's kids bundling home from school. Shrieks of delight. A cacophony of noise that, aside from Zal, was the closest she had come to company since she had moved out of the Real Res – and that was hardly the kind of company she wanted to keep anyway. She imagined everyone on the estate reading Jess's post, pointing up at the twelfth-floor window and laughing at the invisible girl behind it, who only existed online and had no life away from it. Her breath caught in her chest, unable to move up her throat and out of her mouth. She wondered if she would die there, in this Sweet Dreamz bed, all alone, her sole friend in the world a boy she had only met once.

Barb clutched her head but she was too preoccupied with sadness to notice the smooth spot at the crown of her head. Another day it might have registered, but not then. Not yet.

CHAPTER 8

In the days after seeing Jess's post, the jolts came thick and fast. They were completely merciless. Barb couldn't move her head from her pillow without feeling as if she was in freefall. The thought of breakfast felt like climbing Everest to her.

She couldn't fathom going into the kitchen, finding a bowl and a spoon, putting her beloved Weetabix in said bowl, pouring milk over it, and then raising the spoon from the bowl to her mouth. It felt like the kind of thing that other people did, people braver and stronger than her – an astronaut, perhaps, or a deep-sea diver. How could she, Barb, who had nothing but the hair on her head, get out of bed, and make herself breakfast, let alone consider a day that might involve creating content that a quarter of a million people might see? It wasn't so much that the thought appalled her; more that it left her feeling cold and motionless on her #gifted bed.

It struck Barb, as she lay there one morning, that she was completely defenceless against the darkness. She had nothing, absolutely *nothing*, to save her from it. When the jolts and the bad thoughts came, they simply swarmed over her. She had no shield to protect herself from them, no light to switch on and scare them away. No real family to speak of, no real friends, no real hobbies and interests outside that of doing her hair and posting it on the internet. Even her contact with Zal had petered out in recent days, him busy with the buzz that his challenge had created.

Her wardrobe was groaning with free clothes from OKHUN, and her desk was covered in freebies from hair brands: straighteners, curlers, heat-shield sprays and silk hair scrunchies. But the only thing that she owned that actually mattered to her was the picture of her mum next to the Buddha. And even that reminded her that she was a mistake, a deadly mistake at that, and these jolts and this darkness were the fitting karma for what she had done to her mum. She had come into this world faulty, and at no point had she managed to fix the fault. There was something wrong with her – and not in a way that might invite compassion or empathy, those other buzz words she saw all over social media. There was something wrong with her because she *deserved* to have something wrong with her, because she had killed her mum and ruined her aunt's life.

And betrayed Jess.

Nobody posted on their social media accounts about what it felt like to kill their mum in childbirth before they'd barely even taken a breath. Sometimes they posted about feeling low or anxious or being unsure about themselves, but not wrong. Nobody came out and said, 'I think I am a bad person and that I deserve to be punished.' As far as Barb knew, it was just her, alone on the twelfth floor of the Warriner Estate, a lone island of wrongness in a sea of rightness.

She did not dare feel sorry for herself: self-pity would have been an insult to all those whose lives she had ruined.

ONE DAY TO GO

Every day Barb would wait for her aunt to leave for work. It wasn't as if she did much once Sorcha was out the flat; no, it was more that she felt she could at least exist without lying to her aunt that she was locked away in her bedroom creating content, replying to messages, engaging with her audience etc, etc, blah, blah, yada, yada, yada.

But on this particular morning, the sounds of Sorcha clomping around the flat as she got ready for work were suspiciously absent. The sound of Radio 1's breakfast show didn't come blaring through the walls from the kitchen radio, jolting her awake. The white noise of the hair dryer didn't materialise. No doors slammed. No floors knocked under the weight of her towering heels.

It was peaceful. In so much as somewhere *could* be peaceful when your brain was constantly telling you that you were a piece of shit the world stepped around. The kind of peaceful where the only sound is the bombs going off in your head.

Barb tried to breathe deeply. Last night, scrolling sleeplessly in the dark, she had come across the page of an influencer who specialised in 'breathwork'. 'CALM YOUR MIND WITH YOUR OWN PEACEFUL POWER' read the bio, entirely in caps, not particularly calmly. Their page was a series of videos featuring breathing techniques to CALM YOUR MIND. Barb watched three of them, her chest tightening with each not-so-calming encouragement to breathe in through your nose and out through your mouth. The more she had to *think* about breathing, the less she felt able to actually do it. 'Your breath is the key to *everything*,' cooed the creator, as Barb started to feel a little bit woozy.

She realised, suddenly, that she had not actually managed to exhale for the entire duration of the video, that she had been holding her breath from the moment it began.

As Barb lay back on her pillow and put down her phone, she wondered how it was possible for her to even be crap at breathing.

But as she woke to the unexpected silence, the reality

of her life squatting heavily on her chest, she decided to give the breathing a crack. She began to breathe in through her nose. Then she breathed out through her mouth. She did this a few times, amazed that she was actually managing to breathe; other accomplishments, such as eating breakfast or having a shower or getting dressed in something other than pyjamas, would have to wait for now. She breathed iiinnn through her nose, and ooouuut through her mouth; iiinnn through her nose, ooouuut through her mouth; iiin through her—

'BARB!' came a bark from the door. 'What the HELL are you doing? Why didn't you wake me up? I'm bloody late for work now!'

Barb breathed ooouuut through her mouth and sat up. She started to apologise, then wondered when she had become her aunt's human alarm clock. Not that she would ever be so impertinent as to say such a thing. 'Was I supposed to wa—'

'I must have slept through my alarm. Why didn't you tell me? What's the *point* of you if you can't even do that? Honestly, I feel like I spend my whole life trying to accommodate you! I ask *nothing* of you, nothing at all, not even for you to go to school! Most kids would be cock-a-bloody-*hoop* that they lived with an aunt who let them leave school as soon as they turned sixteen! But not you. Not Barb! No, Little Miss Social Media Superstar is too busy moping in her bedroom over some pathetic little video by a girl who has about a hundred and fifty-three followers, as if there was nothing else going on in the world!'

Barb must have looked surprised because Sorcha went into one. 'You think I don't know why you're locked in here all day? You think I'm too naive to see what's going on? You think I don't occasionally look at that loser's little page to see if she's spreading poison about you? Barb, how many times do I have to tell you: SHE DOESN'T MATTER! She's nobody! She has no followers, no life outside this crappy estate, whereas you could have the world at your feet if you play your cards right, if you take the opportunity that's been given to you with your bloody hair. You're just like your mum, you know, just like her. I'm sick of it!'

Sorcha stormed out of the room and Barb allowed herself, for a moment, to wonder how she was like her mum. Her thoughts were interrupted by the reappearance of her aunt, who was now waving her toothbrush in the air. 'And *don't* think it's escaped my notice that you have been chatting with that blind boy, whatshisgob.'

Barb smiled politely at her aunt's wonderful tact. 'You can't let pining for him ruin your career, OK? There's no time for that. You need to be CREATING CONTENT!'

But I'm not pining for Zal, Barb thought, as the door slammed behind Sorcha when she finally left for work. Her aunt had majorly misread the situation (as ever). While everyone was living their best, most peachy lives out there, Barb was the only person in the world – or at least the Warriner Estate – who was such a failure as a human being. 'I'm pining for life.'

But Sorcha was right about Jess: Barb couldn't get the image of Jess and Serena out of her head, nor the comments underneath it. As much as she loathed to admit it, she missed Jess. She needed Jess. And perhaps, she told herself, she needed this reminder from her and Serena that she couldn't just move on from what she had done, and how she had behaved. She needed to be punished, again and again and again.

She needed to be punished for what she had done to Jess, but she also needed to be punished for what she had done to her mother. How dare she think she deserved an outrageously good life when she had denied one to her mum? And Sorcha. She had completely ruined any chance for Sorcha to have an outrageously good life.

It was all Barb had, this hair, and she needed to be grateful that Sorcha was trying to help her make the best of it. She owed it to her aunt to buck up and get up, stop feeling so sorry for herself and create some content.

So that was what she was going to do.

Tomorrow.

Definitely tomorrow.

Today she would just lie in her wrongness for a little

bit longer. *Then I'll gather the strength to get up and on with my life.*

So that's what she did.

D-DAY

When she decided to get on with her life the next day, karma rewarded her with the discovery of the patch.

This is it, she thought, stroking the bald patch. Feeling calm. Feeling the sense of it all. Almost feeling triumphant.

Finally, this is all that I deserve.

CHAPTER 9

It happened quite quickly after that. It was as if, after sixteen years of crushing guilt, her body had finally worked out the most efficient way to punish itself, and now it wasn't going to hang around. That tiny bald patch – unmistakeable, but small, no bigger than a five-pence coin – had grown to the size of a fifty-pence coin within days. Barb was sure of it. And no sooner had she come to terms with it growing to the size of a fifty-pence coin, then it had grown to the size of a five-pound note. And she was convinced that that particular growth had happened over night.

She was also sure that just looking for it with her finger, and then with the camera on her phone, was all the fuel that the bald patch needed to get bigger and bigger and bigger. It was unstoppable. Like a runaway train. Once she had noticed the patch, she couldn't stop noticing it. Every day she spent what seemed like hours, sitting in front of the mirror in her bedroom, combing her hairline this way and that to cover the patch so that she could continue to create the videos that were the only thing that stopped her aunt storming through the door of her bedroom and having a go at her. It was lucky that her hair was so thick – she could pin it in such a way that you'd never know a giant bald patch existed slap bang on the crown of her head.

And so, for a little while, she could carry on as if nothing had happened. As if all was normal and her brief period in bed was just a phase that she had finally broken through thanks to her aunt's stern talking-to.

The patch had given Barb a strange new energy. A purpose even. It was as if she was atoning for all her sins with it. In the days after finding it, Barb created more content than she had in the entire six months previously: Your best New Year's Eve hair yet!; New Year, New Hair styles; a guide to the best dry shampoos; a plait tutorial; a blow dry hacks video; how to make your wash last a week in hairstyles; the best conditioning treatments; do hair gummies work? (this was a brand partnership that Sorcha had arranged, and so of course the answer was: yes, yes they do); holy grail hair products; and finally, hair turbans – yay or nay? (she had to stop herself from saying nay purely because Catrina liked wearing them).

Not once did she look at Jess or Serena's feeds. She didn't even pay much attention to Zal's, too embarrassed that she had only congratulated him on it, rather than actually taking part in it. She couldn't bear the thought of Jess seeing it and thinking it was a response to her post. She noted that Pixie had reappeared, after her brief hiatus, talking about how she had needed a break and how amazingly supportive her friend Catrina had been – her friend who, just a few weeks ago, had been happy to trade her in as a housemate.

Barb watched Pixie's content, wincing. It was as if those few days in the Real Res had never even happened. Pixie had created a reel of pictures of her and Catrina together, an Adele song playing in the background, with captions about the true meaning of friendship. Barb imagined Anna G rubbing her hands in glee at this about-turn, and then promptly put them all out of her mind as a flurry of notifications filled her screen.

Comments were pouring in for her twisted updo video, the one she was filming when she first found the patch. She had edited that stuff out, obviously – she was hardly going to show everyone her bald patch – and put together what she thought was a pretty good twisted updo tutorial. The comments seemed to agree:

'Going to do this for a night out at the weekend!'

'My god your hair is just gorgeous – like you!'

'Your feed is everything.'

'I wish I had hair like yours.'

'Can we be friends?'

And so on and so on – each banal comment requiring at least a like. But she couldn't help noticing the trolls, no matter what Catrina had advised. Given how fake Catrina had turned out to be, she wasn't even sure she should believe anything she said. Was she getting more of them, or was she just feeling particularly vulnerable that day? The trolls were vastly outnumbered by the nice comments, but their venom meant they stuck with her more.

'Ur as fake as ur hair.'

'Zzz nobody cares.'

And, most curiously: 'The only thing that's twisted about this video is that you've got so many likes for it when you're such a sham.'

Barb felt attacked. She felt jolts on her. Even though she knew, deep down, that these comments were coming from random strangers who spent their time scrolling social media being horrible to people, today they felt kind of personal. They made her think back to Jess's video. To Jess's comments. Her accusations of the fakeness of their friendship cut deep. It hurt. To Barb, their friendship had been the most real thing in her life . . . but, increasingly, Barb wasn't sure what the word 'real' meant.

She deleted them all, felt the sweet relief of being able to do this, but it was short lived. As soon as she got rid of one, another would appear:

'@letdownyourhair is such a FAKE she can't even let people comment freely on her page!'

'why are you deleting comments, @letdownyourhair? Got something to hide?'

'more inauthentic crap from you, so sad that you can't even take a little bit of constructive criticism'

She decided to leave them be. She could try limiting comments from these people, but she knew they'd only pop up in some other guise. Switching comments off wasn't an option if she wanted to keep her engagement and, more importantly, her career.

She searched the internet for guides to dealing with trolls. 'Try hiding keywords in comments that might trigger you,' wrote one 'expert'. Barb wondered where she would even start: hair, fake, inauthentic . . . How could she control everyone on social media? How could she stop people from being mean? If she started down that particular road, she knew she would never come off it. She would never spend time doing anything other than policing her comments.

Barb let out a weary sigh and then stroked her five-pound note bald patch for comfort. She sensed once again that the dimensions had changed, that it had continued its spread across her crown. She was just about to explore further when a notification pinged.

Zal!

For a moment, the comments disappeared from her

mind, as did the patch. She went to her inbox and played back the message from Zal.

@IAmZal: 'Glorious human, how are you? Sorry I've been quiet, this whole challenge thing has been kicking off. And don't think I haven't noticed your absence from it . . . Barb, this challenge doesn't need politicians and celebrities, it needs *you*! Anyway, I just wanted to drop you a note because you've been quiet. And we *need* to talk about Pixie and Catrina. Also, the new season of *Derry Girls*. My inbox misses you, @letdownyourhair. *It misses you!* Are you, like, ignoring me?'

Barb felt joy flood through her. She cleared her throat and started to speak into her phone.

@letdownyourhair: 'Hearing your lovely voice is just what I needed—'

No, that wouldn't do. Too keen. She deleted it and started again.

@letdownyourhair: 'Hey, Zal! It's so nice to hear from y—'

She cringed at her own voice. She sounded like a distant cousin doing their annual check-in. She needed to sound warm yet casual. Happy to hear from him, but not *too* happy to hear from him, in a way that might imply he was the only person she ever heard from. She needed him to know that she was . . . She lost her train of thought as she noticed Zal's profile turn green, and another voice note drop into her inbox.

@IAmZal: 'Helloooooo, Barb, I can see you are there. No, that's not true. I can't see that you are there, but my screen reader can. It alerts me when a message has been listened to. It's like my very own personal stalker who I can blame for sounding weird and obsessive. It's not my fault my screen reader feels the need to announce when you've heard one of my voice notes, right? OK! So I'm going now, before I sound *really, really* weird, as opposed to just moderately weird, which is what I'm guessing I sound like right now. GOODBYE!'

Barb laughed. She realised she had no reason to worry about what she sounded like, just that she sounded like something. She started recording.

@letdownyourhair: 'Oh my God, Zal, I am totally calling the police and getting a restraining order on your screen reader. Do you think they would take me seriously? Seriously, though, it's great to hear from you. I've been sitting at home alone with only the trolls and the Derry Girls for company. It's been getting me down if I'm honest, and I feel like I can be honest with you. Also – Pixie and Catrina? How long before they are on a #gifted girls' trip to Dubai, or something?'

@IAmZal: 'Anna G wouldn't let them go to Dubai because of its poor human-rights record. *Keep up.* They will, however, definitely be visiting a relatable yoga retreat that their followers can also visit with a thirty per cent discount using the code AUTHENTICITY4LIFE30. But that is all by the by. What's more important is that you know that whoever is trolling you needs to use the exclusive code GETALIFE123. Seriously, that shit always says more about them than you. Imagine wanting to spend a moment of your one precious life sending nasty comments to someone you don't know.'

Barb welled up at this. He was being so kind, and yet if he only knew the truth, that these people *did* know her and had every reason to send her nasty comments . . . She shook the thoughts from her head and started recording a reply.

@letdownyourhair: 'Can I tell you something that is going to sound completely weird?'

@IAmZal: 'Weirder than the fact that my screen reader is stalking you?'

@letdownyourhair: 'OK. Good point. So you know about my mum and how she died. I guess when I see the nasty comments, they kind of feel familiar to me. They feel like the voice in my own head, the one I use on myself. I feel like such a bad person for what I did to her that in a weird kind of way the trolls make sense.'

She almost added that to add to her general confusion, her hair had started falling out. But in the silence that ensued as he recorded, she chickened out. She'd burdened him with enough for one day.

@IAmZal: 'Barb, babes, this is such a sad thing to hear.

You didn't do anything to your mum. It's not your fault that she died. I mean, I don't want to sound like the teenager I am, but you didn't ask to be born. I totally said that to my mum every day the year I turned fourteen. No word of a lie. Anyway, you couldn't have stopped what happened. It was just really, really bad luck. You know what someone who has had really, really bad luck needs? They need to talk to themselves kindly. Oh, man, did you hear the cliché that just came out of my mouth? But it's cliché for a reason, and that reason is because it's *true*! I hate that you are basically trolling yourself every day. We all get trolls. Even Pixie and Catrina get trolls. *Especially* Pixie and Catrina. They just have assistants at Spark Enterprises whose job it is to go around scrubbing out any evidence of said trolls' existence. Do you think Pixie did that video the other night because social media is a fundamentally good place full of good people who just want the best for you? No. It's a cesspit. A toxic cesspit.'

@letdownyourhair: 'I'm trying not to, but it's so hard to ignore it, you know? Five hundred nice comments, five horrid ones, and guess which ones I'm focusing on?'

@IAmZal: 'Do you know, it's actually a really understandable reaction. Have you heard of negativity bias? Stop listening if you have, but focusing on the bad stuff at the expense of the good is actually an evolutionary thing. It's the only reason any of us are alive today. If we didn't do that, God wouldn't have created the internet and chat rooms and we wouldn't be talking right now. *Imagine that, Barb! Imagine that!* How it works is, like, way back at the dawn of time when our ancestors were living on the African plains and they had no social media or Wi-Fi, even, they had to remember the negative things about their environment to stop themselves from getting killed. Like, don't go near that cave – a lion lives there and it will eat me. Or stay away from that settlement – there's a hostile tribe who will stick a spear through my brain. Or don't eat that leaf – it's poison. That kind of thing. Prioritising the bad stuff over the good stuff kept us alive back then. But now, with Wi-Fi and social media, it actually stops us from living. It stops us from getting to the good stuff we deserve. That you deserve. Don't let the trolls stop you from evolving, Barb. Focus on the good stuff and you'll be OK.'

Barb breathed deeply. Iiinnn through her nose, ooouuut through her mouth. For a moment it actually worked. She started speaking into her phone again.

@letdownyourhair: 'You know what? You're the good stuff, Zal. You're the good stuff.'

And then she pressed send, instead of delete.

CHAPTER 10

The patch had got bigger. Much bigger. Barb imagined it like Pac-Man, chomping through the follicles on her head. A few weeks ago it was a five-pound note, but now it was more like a twenty. The white skin of her scalp was now so noticeable that it would be difficult to film any content from above her head without it showing. It contrasted quite starkly with the peach of her hair, a sort of reverse sunburn. Barb was a whizz at camera angles but even she would struggle to conceal it without resorting to some serious photo-editing software. But she had made enough content to buy herself time. Time to find out what was wrong with her.

And yet there was the constant nagging feeling that what was wrong with her was actually what was right with her. She couldn't help but feel strangely *grateful*. If it carried on growing at the rate it did, Sorcha's entire plan for her would completely burn to the ground. She was nothing without her hair. Jess had told her that months ago.

But she couldn't help but wonder . . . what would it be like to be nothing?

What would it be like to have her slate wiped completely clean so she had to start all over again? She could be whoever she wanted to be instead of the person she was supposed to be. She could tell her own story instead of acting out the one that had been written for her.

Barb looked at the photo of the patch on her phone and then deleted it so that Sorcha would never see it. She shook the wild thoughts from her head. As if she could break free from this woman who had done everything for her since the day she was born. As if she could make anything of herself without her hair. It was the only thing that stood between her and complete oblivion. What was she without her social media, her followers, or her aunt? Without any of these things, she might as well not exist.

Whatever was causing this blossoming bald patch, she had to stop it as soon as possible. The facts were simple and stark: Barb could not be a successful hair influencer without any hair.

She channelled all her energy into researching what might be causing it. She started by typing words like 'hair falling out' into Google, but she realised that this didn't quite capture what was happening. Her hair wasn't falling out. It wasn't appearing in clumps in her hairbrush, or in huge tangles that clogged up the drains. It was simply ceasing to exist. It was just . . . disappearing. One day it would be there and the next it wasn't.

Anyway, googling 'hair falling out' didn't actually bring up much information – just heaps of products that promised thick and lustrous hair.

'Hair falling out? Try our amazing ginger scalp treatment and see results fast!'

'Transform your hair with Gorgeous Beauty Hair Vitamins!'

'Hair thinning and shedding? THIS IS THE PRODUCT YOU NEED RIGHT NOW'

'THE REAL REASON YOU ARE STRUGGLING TO GROW YOUR HAIR . . .'

Barb thought she might cry. These weren't solutions, just empty promises designed to enrich some arsehole somewhere, but not her scalp. She knew because she did this herself. The hair gummies paid-partnership post popped into her head. She popped it back out again, as she seemed to be doing with so many thoughts nowadays.

'Bald patch on head woman' provided a little more in the way of information. 'ALOPECIA AREATA is patchy hair loss that happens suddenly on the head or the body.' This was the first result, placed so prominently on the page that it offered itself like an official diagnosis. She clicked on the related questions in the search engine. 'What causes bald patches in women's hair?' The answer made interesting reading: 'Female pattern baldness is largely thought to occur due to genetics. However, it may also develop due to an underlying condition that affects the production of the hormone androgen. Androgen is a hormone that plays a role in pattern baldness.'

Pattern baldness sounded to Barb like something that happened to men in their sixties, not girls who had just turned sixteen. She carried on.

'Why do I have a bald spot on my head out of nowhere?'

'Bald spots of the scalp, brow, or beard are commonly caused by a medical condition called alopecia areata. It is also commonly called spot baldness, and it is believed to be an autoimmune disorder that causes the body's immune system to mistake hair follicles for foreign invaders, and then attack them as such.'

Barb felt briefly relieved that she didn't have a beard, and then worried about her eyebrows falling out too. As her panic rose, so did the intensity of her searches.

'BALD PATCHES WILL I LOSE ALL MY HAIR?' told her, almost too calmly, that: 'sometimes severe small bald patches develop and merge into a larger bald area. Patches of body hair, beard, eyebrows or eyelashes may be affected in some cases, but this is unusual . . . Some people lose all their scalp hair. This is called alopecia totalis.'

Barb carried on clicking. She clicked and she clicked and she clicked, like a detective in a movie nobody wanted to see. 'Do you always lose all of your hair with alopecia?' told her that: 'Alopecia areata can grow into another form of alopecia. In its worst form, alopecia universalis causes you to lose all body hair. This includes eyebrows, eyelashes, arms, legs, underarms and pubic hair, and chest and back hair for men.' She gulped back hard and thought the feeble need to make a joke about it not being so bad to lose your underarm or pubic hair. Then she remembered she had nobody to make the joke to. Her investigations continued.

'How quickly does alopecia universalis progress?' was a particularly futile line of questioning, given that nobody on the internet seemed to have an answer for it. 'You may start off with small patches of hair loss. These patches spread over time until the entire head is bald. Hair loss can begin suddenly and occur rapidly.'

'HOW DO YOU CURE ALOPECIA' was bleak in its response, but to the point: 'There is currently no cure for alopecia areata.'

Barb had started to breathe deeply without even realising it. Iiinnn through her nose, ooouuut through her mouth. It was as if her subconscious was trying to keep her upright. She read on.

'There are some forms of treatment that can be prescribed

by doctors to help hair regrow more quickly. The most common form of alopecia areata treatment is the use of corticosteroids, powerful anti-inflammatory drugs that can suppress the immune system.'

Barb knew what she had to do. She had to call the doctor.

Barb had worked out that she had precisely six days' worth of content made before she ran out. It was important she was very precise with this because she couldn't risk Sorcha nosing around. She had to keep her happy and pacified, like an overfed baby, in order to have any chance of making things work.

She searched around for the number for her local GP. She wasn't sure she even had one – she couldn't remember the last time she had needed to go to the doctor. Sure, there had been many times when she *should* have gone to one – childhood fevers that blazed for days on end, the times late at night when she found she couldn't breathe properly, episodes that made her think she was dying of a heart attack when she now realised it was more likely the only thing that had been attacking her was panic – but that would have required making a bit of a fuss. And Sorcha didn't like it when she made a bit of a fuss. So instead she'd kept quiet and pushed through in dizzy silence.

Online, Barb found the details of a GP a few streets away. She called. It rang and then put her in a queue, informing her she was eighth in line. Knowing that Sorcha was safely at work, she put the phone on speaker and paced the flat as she waited to make her slow progress to the front of the queue. Five minutes passed. Then ten. Finally, a bored-sounding woman came on the line, asking her if she wouldn't mind holding.

Barb wanted to scream, 'NOOO! I can't hold on any longer! I need help NOW or my life is pretty much over!' But that would have required a certain amount of spunk that she simply didn't possess. Instead, she whispered an 'OK' and went back to pacing the room. Another few minutes passed, and then the line went dead.

She called back and repeated the entire process again. After forty-five minutes, she finally got through to a human who didn't want to put her back in an automated queue. 'Hello, welcome to Warriner Estate Medical Practice, sorry for the wait, how can I be of assistance to you?'

Barb was suddenly hit by the absolute vanity of what she was doing. She was calling a doctor's surgery that helped properly ill people because her hair wasn't as nice as it had previously been. But she couldn't back out now, not after she'd come this far. She did some of that breathing she was getting so much better at. Iiinnn through the nose, outttttt through the mouth. Then she spoke. 'Hi, I think I need an appointment with the doctor. There's something wrong with my head.'

As Barb said the words, she immediately regretted saying them.

'I'm sorry, dear. It's very common for people to have mental health problems. It's nothing to be ashamed of and you've absolutely done the right thing calling toda—'

'No, no, I don't mean a mental health thing,' Barb said, interrupting someone for what she realised was the first time in her entire life. 'I'm sorry, that was really very rude of me. But what I mean is, there's something *physically* wrong with my head. Like, my hair is disappearing. And I know that sounds really vain but I need help. I don't know what to do.'

The woman remained quiet on the other end. Barb imagined her rolling her eyes with impatience. She finally broke the silence. 'Can I ask, have you tried going to your hairdresser? Because it seems like that might be a more appropriate place than a busy GP practice.'

Barb breathed iiinnn. And then she breathed outtttt.

'Actually, I have,' she lied, 'and they said it was something I needed to see the doctor about. So please can you arrange that for me?'

She didn't know where *this* version of herself was coming from, but she kind of liked it.

The woman tutted and then sighed. 'Can I take your

name, please? And then I can get you booked in for an appointment.'

Barb pumped her fist in the air, fully aware that nobody but her could see this small gesture of victory. 'Yes, it's Barbara McDonnell. M-C-D-O-N-N-E-L-L.' In the background, she heard tapping on a keyboard.

'Can you say that again?' asked the woman on the other end of the phone.

Barb said it again. And then another time, for luck. But it was no use – it was as if the communication had officially broken down between the two of them. Was the woman already in a dream world where she was regaling her colleagues with tales of Barb's vanity?

'I'm sorry, Miss McDonnell, but you don't seem to be on our system. Could it be that you have another name?'

Barb realised that she did – @letdownyourhair – but this was unlikely to be what the receptionist meant. 'I think it's because I'm not registered,' blurted out Barb.

'OK, dear. You sound awfully young and more than a little bit anxious, I have to say.' Barb wanted to respond that she sounded awfully old and more than a little bit unhelpful, but she had used up all her ballsyness for the time being. 'Do you mind me asking if your parents know that you're ringing?'

Barb did mind. She minded very much that she had to constantly explain her circumstances, that every day she ran up against these seemingly trivial things that poked more holes in her soul. And she minded very much that she was supposed not to mind. It was exhausting, this not minding. It was like constantly carrying the weight of an elephant and pretending it was enjoyable. And she'd had enough of it.

'Actually, my parents don't know that I'm ringing you because they are dead. And I'm sixteen, so I don't need anyone's permission to register for a doctor. So if we could just get on with it, that would be grand.'

And for the first time in Barb's life, someone did as she said.

In the end, Barb's uncharacteristic outburst had served her quite well. Not only had the woman registered her quickly but she had even given Barb an 'emergency' appointment that afternoon. The doctor would video call between 2 p.m. and 3 p.m. This pleased Barb, who did not want to leave the flat or come face to face with this woman she had just been so bolshy to. She might die of shame.

At two minutes to three, the phone rang. Barb felt sick to her stomach as she pressed accept.

The doctor on the other end was a woman whose distractedness was clear even through the fuzzy pixels of FaceTime. 'Hello, Barbara,' she sighed. 'I'm Dr Crawley. How can I help you today?'

You could help me by giving me some drugs to get my hair back, Barb thought. *You could help me by giving my aunt some drugs so she doesn't notice that my hair is disappearing.*

'I, I . . .' Barb tried to do the breathing. 'I am going bald and I'm only sixteen years old. And a girl. And it may seem vain but my hair is really important to me. It's sort of how I earn a living. So I really need help getting it back.'

Dr Crawley seemed unimpressed. 'Your hair looks fine to me,' she replied. 'Lovely, actually. I would have died for hair like that when I was your age. Can you show me where the problem is?'

So Barb showed her. She moved the camera of the phone to the back of her head and . . .

'Oh, I see.' Dr Crawley appeared chastened. Was Barb finally getting somewhere? 'Gosh, you'd never know from looking at you, would you? How lucky you are to have all that fabulous thick hair to cover it!'

Now Barb felt chastened, as if she was making a mountain out of a molehill. She tried to hold it together. This was not the reaction she had expected from the GP – although, given the receptionist's reaction earlier, she didn't know why.

'I'm glad you can see it, Dr Crawley,' she said. 'But I wondered if you could give me something for it. I think it might be alopecia, and I read somewhere that there's medication that helps with it.'

181

'Have you been experiencing any itchiness?' Dr Crawley asked, ignoring Barb's self-diagnosis.

'No,' Barb replied.

'Any discomfort?'

'N-n-no – well, no physical discomfort.'

'It does look like alopecia to me,' said Dr Crawley after a short pause. 'The thing is, I don't like prescribing medication for things that aren't actually making you unwell. There's no itching or rash as far as I can see, and it's not like alopecia can actually harm you. I'd rather we look at some natural solutions first, such as nutrition and exercise. Have you tried meditating? That might be good to calm your nerves about it.'

Barb felt remarkably similar to how she had felt when she watched Jess's video. It was a sense of humiliation, with a large dollop of shame mixed in for good measure. She felt embarrassed and trivial. She nodded along to Dr Crawley's words, as if this might minimise her sense of embarrassment.

'Miss McDonnell, alopecia is more common than you'd think. Often it's hormonal. You are sixteen, an age where you have to deal with a lot: exams and school and whatnot. In my experience, stress is responsible for most cases of alopecia, and when you remove the stress, the patches will start to go. Has anything stressful happened to you recently? Do you have a history of stress or depression?

Has something bad happened in the past that might have contributed to this?'

But Barb had gone back to her usual quiet self. It seemed pointless, really, to respond. She only had two minutes of Dr Crawley's time left and where would she even begin?

CHAPTER 11

Jess had made another video, this time thanking all her followers for their support. Barb only knew this because that night, Sorcha returned from work and came straight into Barb's room – as ever, without knocking – brandishing her phone and with a look of something approaching completely unbridled joy on her face.

'You will never guess WHAT, Barbie.' Her aunt waved the phone a bit more. Barb, who had covered her hair in a brightly coloured OKHUN silk-effect headscarf in preparation for her aunt's return, expected some sort of announcement about a new brand partnership, so it was a surprise when she brought up Jess's tear-stained face on the screen of her phone.

'This girl! The bloody *cheek of her*! She's done a video *thanking* her followers for all their support following her last video.'

As Sorcha pressed the play sign on the centre of Jess's big, emotional face, it occurred to Barb that her aunt was actually enjoying this. Bringing her this bad news was giving Sorcha some sort of sick, twisted kick, a thrill far bigger than any good news she could deliver about partnerships with shampoo brands or hair spray manufacturers.

In the video Jess was talking directly to the camera as the tears had begun to flow.

Barb didn't think she could ever cry on camera, but then she remembered that she was a failure of a human and this probably said more about her than it did about Jess.

Her former best friend wiped a tear from below her eyes which, Barb noticed, had been beautifully made up but did not seem to have been affected one jot by the tears. Had Jess persuaded her dad to let her have eyelash extensions? God, stuff *had* changed since they'd fallen out.

'Guys, I'm so sorry to clog up your feeds with more videos of me baring my soul' - she sniffed delicately - 'but I just wanted to thank you all for your incredible support over that video I did as part of Zal's amazing challenge. It was a bit of a risk putting it out there; I felt really vulnerable' - she sniffed and chewed her lip emotionally - 'but as I'm finding out, being vulnerable is the only way to live your life authentically. I wish I'd done it earlier in many ways. And I want you to know that you can be vulnerable, too.' She closed her eyes as if in a sort of reverie. Then she opened them and smiled softly. 'You don't have to be alone in this,' she said, shaking her head in what Barb assumed was supposed to be a compassionate way. 'If you need me, I'm here for you like you've been for me.'

The video ended, 'PLAY AGAIN' appearing across Jess's face.

Sorcha let out a near-hysterical laugh. 'Hollywood, here she comes! Oh my goodness, my sides are aching from watching this, Barb. She's such a FAKE! She's going on like she's Catrina but she's only got about thirty-two followers – as if any of them are glued to their feeds waiting for her to post her vulnerability!' There was another cackle.

Barb conceded that Jess would probably do well in the Real Res. But she also felt strangely protective of Jess in that moment. She didn't like to see her ex-BFF cry, even if it did look a bit put on for the camera. She hated that social media turned everybody into critics when nobody – not Sorcha and certainly not Barb any more – had any idea what was going on in Jess's life.

'Well, you're clearly glued to her feed because you've seen it,' said Barb, perhaps a little too hypocritically given that she was not above this behaviour herself.

'Only so you don't have to be. I only check in from time to time so you can get on with your life and not waste it *stalking* her.' Sorcha sighed and sat down on the bed next to Barb.

Barb instinctively moved away. 'Don't say that, Sorcha.' She felt a sting of shame pass through her. 'I don't stalk her, OK? I just sometimes look because we used to be best friends and then suddenly we weren't and it's hard to just get over that.'

For a moment, Sorcha really looked at Barb. In the way someone who cared might. In the way a mother might. Then she shook the look away and pulled her face back into her familiar grinning grimace. 'All right, kiddo, no need to get all sensitive on me.' She laughed off Barb's concerns, swept them away under the gifted bed. 'And, more importantly, you need to tell me what the *hell* you have on your head there?'

Barb was glad of the change of subject, not least because it allowed her to put her plan into action – the plan that would buy her even more time so she could somehow get her hands on those steroid things and get her hair to grow back. She smiled sweetly at her aunt and then launched into the speech she had been preparing ever since she got off the phone to Dr Crawley earlier.

'It's a OKHUN scarf. But I thought I could adapt it into a head scarf and do some fashion content – you know, dirty hair days, day-before-wash styles, that kind of thing. Thought it would please OKHUN and make up for that little blip we had with Spark.' She framed her scarf-covered head with her hands as if posing for a camera. 'What do you think?'

Barb knew immediately that her plan was not going to come off in the way she had hoped. Sorcha looked at her as if she had just suggested shaving her hair off for charity, letting out another hysterical laugh that filled the silence like artillery fire.

'What I think, Barb, is that people follow you so they *don't* have to wear scarves on their heads.' She puffed out her cheeks in astonishment at her niece's bad judgement. 'They follow you because they want to show their hair off, not hide it under some cheap bit of polyester that's probably going to make it stand on end with static as soon as you take it off, no matter how much grease there is on it. What I *think* Barb, is that you look ridiculous.' She shook her head, laughed again, and then, in a moment that Barb could see coming but was somehow powerless to stop, she pulled the scarf from her niece's head.

Sorcha McDonnell was not a cryer: in fact, it was a matter of considerable pride to her and one that she liked to point out to Barb on any occasion, as if her inability to shed tears was the emotional equivalent of an Olympic medal. Sorcha didn't have many beliefs but her view on crying was strong enough to make up for this: Sorcha thought that tears were a waste of precious energy and, what was worse, they only ruined your make-up. Nothing was worth ruining your make-up for in Sorcha's mind.

'No use crying over someone like that,' Sorcha had snapped when she had found Barb crying in her bedroom after things had gone wrong with Jess. She had rolled her eyes to the heavens at that pathetic display of emotion. 'You need the energy for more important things like *living your best life!*' She had sashayed to a seated position next to her niece. 'Honestly, why dehydrate over someone so petty? If she was a real friend, Barb, she'd be happy for you.'

Barb had stopped crying not because she wanted to but because the presence of her aunt was like a sort of emotional freeze sweeping in from icy wastelands. It was impossible to express anything around her other than compliant agreement. She supposed that in its own strange way, this *was* Sorcha's way of providing comfort, but there were times when she could have done with a good cry and a slab of chocolate. Still, that was not her aunt's way. Of course there had been the hangover episode after the party. But those tears turned out to be entirely manipulative.

'Barb, do you think I cried when I found my mum dead on the kitchen floor? *Nope!* I had a sister to deal with and just had to get on with it. And do you think I cried when she died? *Nope!* I had a baby niece to deal with and just had to get on with it. Tears are a luxury that people like us can't afford. I'd rather spend my energy moving onwards and upwards!'

But Sorcha cried now as she tried to process the mess that was Barb's scalp. Her whole body shook with the sobs that came pouring out of her mouth and her nose and her eyes, sobs so powerful that they even dislodged Sorcha's trusty waterproof mascara. It was as if her aunt had been possessed by some strange spirit who was intent on releasing all the tears she had previously refused to shed.

Barb had no idea what to say. All she could do was witness it like the momentous occasion it was.

Besides which, the tears were better than what had come before.

Sorcha had tugged at Barb's headscarf and revealed the bald patches that now swamped the whole of the top of her niece's head. She had let out a wail so pained that at first Barb thought it might have been coming from an emergency vehicle on the streets outside. Then she had started grabbing at what remained of Barb's hair, lifting it up as if to check that Barb wasn't playing a prank on her.

Instinctively Barb had pulled away, which had only made Sorcha tug at it all the more. It was painful, almost an act of violence, and yet Barb knew that this was her aunt's way of showing her love. 'WHAT HAVE YOU DONE TO YOURSELF?' Sorcha had continued to wail, pulling Barb's hair this way and that so she could see the full extent of her scalp. 'HOW COULD YOU DO THIS TO US? I know you hate me, but this is taking things to extremes!'

'I haven't done anything, Sorch!' Barb stood up and moved away from her aunt. How could Sorcha think she hated her? 'I wanted to tell you earlier but I thought I could maybe sort it out and then I wouldn't have to bother you with it. I know how busy you've been.' She paused, realising her cheeks were also wet with tears. 'I'd never do anything to hurt you.'

But Sorcha didn't appear to be listening. 'YOUR HAIR!' she wailed. 'Your beautiful hair! It's all we've got! And you've ruined it! YOU'VE RUINED IT!'

Barb almost pitched backwards on to the bed with the force of the screams. And then her aunt suddenly collapsed on the floor, her body juddering as if possessed.

Barb knelt down beside her. 'Sorch? Sorch?' She wondered if she was having some sort of seizure, and if she was now going to be personally responsible for someone *else's* demise. 'Sorcha!' she exclaimed, her tears falling down her cheeks like a raging river. 'Are you OK? What's happening?'

A perfect calm seemed to come over her aunt's body. She stopped shaking. She stopped crying. She lay very still for a moment that felt like an eternity, and then she looked up at Barb with something fiery and frightening in her eyes. It was the kind of look Barb had only seen once before – the night when it all ended with Jess.

Barb pulled some tear-soaked strands of hair from her

face and moved back, away from her aunt.

Sorcha stood up, dusted herself down, and wiped a smudge of mascara from her face. Just as quickly as the demon had possessed her, it had left. 'Don't think you're going to get away with this,' she snarled, turning and walking towards the door. Then she shot Barb one last look – one of hatred. 'I'm DAMNED if you're going to mess everything up for me.'

CHAPTER 12

For almost a month Barb didn't speak to a single soul. It was a record, even for her. She switched off her phone and her voice fell completely silent. Even the DPD delivery driver seemed to have vanished, as if everyone already knew that Barb's – or Sorcha's – dream had well and truly bitten the dust, causing her to be automatically deleted from the list of creators worth sending boxes of tat to.

This list didn't exist, of course, but Barb thought it might as well. She imagined it in a sort of *Matrix*-type world, monitored by all-seeing and all-powerful machines who would unplug a creator the moment they became irrelevant or old hat. Sorcha had once made her watch that movie when she was about eight. She'd described it as 'bonding time', and Barb had leapt at the opportunity, not because *The Matrix* was a 15 certificate, which seemed wildly grown-up to her back then, but because it was a sign her aunt actually wanted to spend time with her. Of course, thinking back to that movie, with its strange science-fiction sex, Barb could now see that it was an entirely inappropriate decision by Sorcha.

And as she lay in her bed in the days after that awful moment with her aunt, she began to ponder just how much else she might have normalised. She had always seen Sorcha's support and encouragement to do social media as a loving thing, but as Barb worried what remained of her hair round her index finger, she couldn't help but think that maybe Sorcha didn't always have her niece's best interests at heart. There was no denying that her aunt had sacrificed a lot to look after Barb . . . but did she really need to sacrifice even more of her life to help her increase her followers and engagement on social media? Wouldn't it have been better to encourage Barb to get some proper qualifications, to join a boring local community group and make some friends? Then Barb could have moaned and whinged like a normal teenager before begrudgingly accepting that her aunt was probably right to keep her in education and knew better than she did.

Lying there, balding, with not a friend in the world or a qualification to her name, she couldn't help but think that maybe, just maybe, her aunt didn't have a clue.

Barb imagined so much during those days, partly because it was all that was left to her once she had switched off her phone and shut it away in her drawer. She couldn't bring herself to look at social media so she hadn't even spoken to Zal. She had thought about telling him what had happened, but she was worried that it would sound vain or trifling compared to what he was doing. And as for her followers, she assumed they had forgotten her by now, or left. She didn't even care. If anything, she liked the idea because it would be exactly what she deserved for all she had put everyone through.

So she lay there, imagining. This was her fate now. To live a life almost entirely in her imagination. She imagined family units where the adults nurtured the children because they loved them, and not because they expected something from them. She imagined experiencing relationships, rather than transactions. She imagined walking freely through the streets with friends, just another teenage girl with teenage-girl struggles like exams and sex and what she might do with the rest of her life.

She had never allowed herself to think about anything as grown-up as sex, mostly because she was scared of messing up her hair. But now, she fantasised about sex. About kissing and touching and sweating; about breathing in someone else's flesh rather than observing their pixellated, filtered pretend lives. She fantasised about all the things she had never experienced in life. Most of all, she fantasised about a life where she didn't have to worry about her bloody hair.

Perhaps two hundred years from now, someone would break open the door of her bedroom and find the husk of her under the bedclothes, a skeleton that nobody had loved or cared enough about to clear away. They would take her bones away and remove what little possessions she owned so they could try to determine more about this peculiar skeleton of the Warriner Estate.

Barb could get quite carried away with this fantasy about her demise. She pictured a futuristic press conference, beamed into people's heads in the normal twenty-third century style. 'We found an early twenty-first century communication device,' they would say when announcing their findings. 'It's a primitive "mobile phone", as was common at the time. And what we have discovered from it is that the skeleton was what was known then as a "creator".' People would ooh and aah as they might these days had they just been told a fascinating historical fact about the Anglo-Saxons. 'Nowadays, it may be perfectly normal for most people to have upwards of a million followers on their telepathic streams, but back then, you were considered important if you had more than a few thousand on your communication device, as was the case with this person. She was very well known on a platform called ShowReal, which was one of the earliest forebears of today's telepathic streams. She would post about how to style your hair.' Pause. Peals of laughter from the audience.

'I know, I know. It seems trifling to us now, in an age when technology allows us to look any way we want, when we can broadcast our thoughts to the world without even touching a button. But back then this was considered quite *advanced* technology. It seems that the Warriner Skeleton had a reasonable amount of popularity until, unfortunately, her hair fell out. Back then you couldn't just get laser treatment and watch it grow back immediately, in the colour and length of your choice. Remember these were people who were really having to live with very, very rudimentary forms of technology, who had none of the things we take for granted today. So sadly for her, that was the end of her career.

'Notes taken from her phone suggest that she lived alone in her bedroom for many years without any friends or family for company, until dying of natural causes at an old age. It's obviously unthinkable for any of us to experience loneliness today, or any other undesirable emotion. And it gives us some insight into how awful loneliness might have felt when I tell you that we were probably the first people to interact with her body since that awful moment when she lost all her hair.'

Barb was quite impressed by how fully fleshed this strange anti-fantasy became in her head during her ten days of silence.

The inspirational quotes her aunt had plastered on the walls felt more mocking than ever. 'Life is not about waiting for the storm to pass, but dancing in the rain' seemed particularly laughable now as she sat miserable and alone in her room, under her own personal storm cloud, without so much as a waterproof coat or an umbrella to protect her from the storm. She had a vague idea of the time, if only from the sounds on the street below her – the shrieking kids and later, the drunks coming back from The Secret Garden. Otherwise she didn't draw the curtain and couldn't have said if it was night or day. Time became yet another abstract construct to her, like friendship or family or normality.

Sorcha wasn't even leaving her Post-it notes any more, which told Barb all she needed to know about the level of her fury. Barb only heard her clunking around the flat as she came and went to work.

Barb added a new anti-fantasy to her store, a scene in which Sorcha had bumped into Jess and Serena outside The Secret Garden and offered to buy them a drink so they could compare notes on the awfulness of Barb. In Barb's mind, they were down there right now, bonding over the shared misfortune that was having to deal with Barbara McDonnell. Perhaps Anna G and Catrina could join them and they could all have a good laugh about the screw-up that used to be @letdownyourhair.

Used to be, because there wasn't that much hair to let down any more. Or even to put up. Barb hadn't dared to look in the mirror since that fateful encounter with her aunt, which had left her feeling like some monstrous freak. She had avoided her own gaze every time she went to the bathroom to go to the loo or brush her teeth. (Had she brushed her teeth today? She couldn't remember, and realised it didn't matter anyway.) But she didn't need a mirror to tell her that the bald patches had progressed, that they were behind her ears and at the nape of her neck and front and centre of her hairline, just above her increasingly wrinkled forehead. She could feel them any time she liked – and she liked to feel them quite a lot.

They had become a strange sort of comfort to her, the only thing able to soothe her and keep away the jolts. How long had she spent lying on her bed, stroking the bald patches that now covered her head? She had no idea. It was an odd thing to have turned into a comfort blanket, but she supposed there wasn't an excess of reassuring presences in her life and that it would have to do.

On what was the thirtieth day – not that Barb had any idea what week, month or year she was now in – she woke to the usual sounds coming from outside her bedroom. The radio blared, the hairdryer revved into life and the kettle bubbled away happily. So far, so normal. Then, just as Barb expected to hear her aunt slam the front door in fury and leave for work, she heard instead the unmistakeable sound of the handle on her *own* bedroom door.

'GET UP!' came a shriek, as Barb pushed her head above the duvet. 'Up, up, up! That's enough moping from you.' Sorcha strode into the bedroom and made her way to the windows, drawing the curtains and blinding Barb with the light. She stood in front of the bed and tutted at her niece.

'Honestly.' She sighed. 'Look at the state of you. Your hair's just got worse and worse, hasn't it? I thought that leaving you to rest for a bit might do you some good, but it's been a month now and it's clearly had no effect. Anyway, no point dwelling on the negatives, although clearly you have been.' She shook her head, then sat down at the end of Barb's bed. 'You know, Barb, all I've ever wanted is the best for you, which is why I'm not letting this period of self-indulgent moping carry on any more. Yes, there's clearly something wrong with you.'

She paused and Barb tried not to congratulate her aunt for working out what she had known for many years now. 'I should have been more sympathetic, really. I mean, I really believed that you had done this to yourself to spite me. But it was a real shock seeing you like that.' Another pause, as she cleared her throat. 'Seeing you like this, I suppose. I needed time to process it and work out what we are going to do. Luckily for you, I've come up with a plan that doesn't involve hiding all the patches under synthetic crap. Do you want to hear it?'

Barb nodded silently, in a way that she hoped at least *looked* enthusiastic.

'OK, so I spoke to Juan and Caz, but obviously I have made them promise not to tell anyone. Because if it got out that you now looked like Dr Evil in *Austin Powers*, we'd be finished. Anyway, obviously I didn't understand what had happened to your hair, but I described it to them and they said it sounded a bit like alopecia.' She struggled to get the word out. 'A-lo-pe-cia,' she repeated. 'Almost sounds as funny as it looks. Apparently, they see it quite a lot in some of the poor sods that come in to get their hair done. Obviously, as the manager, I'm oblivious to it because I'm not getting down and dirty on the salon floor. But anyway, they said it's bad, right, but not completely terrible, cos they've heard there's a few things you can do, and they know a few people who can try and cover it up, right? Apparently, if you get a really good hair extension specialist, we can have you back to normal in no time, making videos, and nobody need ever know that underneath it all you're balder than Bruce Willis.' She let out a shrill laugh at her joke.

'And also, Juan said that you're probably not getting enough vitamins and minerals in your body. I said to him, "You're telling me!" The work I have to do to get you to eat proper food and not just that Weetabix crap. Anyway, I got you these.' She reached into her pocket and pulled out a jar of expensive-looking pills. 'They are worth seventy quid a month! Would you believe it? I've told the company we'll do a post about them and they've gifted us three months free as a result. Which means we have three months to come up with some way to promote the product without revealing why we're using it. But we'll worry about that later.

'Now, I want you to get up, shower, get dressed, and try and make yourself presentable. Even if it involves having to put this on.' She threw a pink beanie hat at the bed with OKHUN's logo on the front of it. 'Then we're going to meet the magician who's going to sort this mess out, work out how to explain your little absence to your followers and get on with our lives as planned. *Comprende?*'

Barb nodded. After all, it wasn't as if she had a choice.

CHAPTER 13

In the time that Barb's phone had been switched off in a drawer, her social media engagement had flatlined. Everything she had spent the last months carefully building had dropped off a cliff in just thirty days. She had stopped playing the game and it had ploughed ahead without her, so that it seemed almost impossible to get back in it. This was the truth, she was realising, about the career she had chosen: it was a full-time job, with no holiday or sick days, and woe betide you should you need some time off.

She thought back to the careers day that Queenstown Academy had put on for its year-eleven students towards the end of her time there. Like most things at school, she had barely paid attention. She knew what she wanted to do and so she had switched off as she was encouraged to take quizzes to find the right career for her, or listen to dull talks from experts about vocational courses and the importance of job security. She was fifteen and had no interest in pensions, or learning the difference between being self-employed or an employee. All she really cared about was getting the hell out of the school gates so she could escape the death stares of Jess and Serena, and the endless feeling of loneliness.

She remembered that hopeful day when she turned sixteen, when she had bounded up the stairs of her tower block, full of the possibility of the rest of her outrageously good life. But now, almost a year on, it wasn't as if she had succeeded. She had barely left the flat since that day and her only friend existed purely online – and she was in danger of losing even him given that she had spent the last month self-indulgently moping.

And now, as she stared at her social media analytics, she saw that it had all been for nothing, that she probably *should* have stayed at school and listened a bit more so that she could have got some proper qualifications and the prospect of a proper job. Her analytics made grim viewing. Not only was her engagement down two hundred per cent, but she had actually lost followers during her absence. No matter that several hundred thousand still remained; she had lost exactly 1,433 followers to be precise. She imagined each and every one of them marching away from her feed in disgust as they realised what a waste of time she was. 'Come on!' they said to each other. 'Let's go and follow some accounts that are actually making a difference rather than one showing us how to brush our hair!'

As the year had gone on, and her numbers had got bigger, so had her fear of losing them all. Extra followers hadn't made her more secure in what she was doing – Barb was realising that the more she relied on her follower numbers, the less she was able to rely on herself. When she looked at these analytics, she felt that they weren't just a reflection of her social-media account, but of her very being. She realised with a jolt, that if she had any self-worth at all, it was invested here in her feed, and she had been careless with that investment, leaving it to flounder as she moped under the duvet cover.

She had stopped giving the algorithm attention for less than a month, and now the algorithm was punishing her with the kind of data that showed she was failing: graphs that plummeted down, down, down, and statistics that were in minus figures.

Her strange anti-fantasy about becoming the Warriner Skeleton wasn't as far-fetched as she had thought. With figures like this, @letdownyourhair, or Barb, or whoever she was, might as well have been dead because nobody was looking at her, or paying her any attention.

Barb felt the jolts, her heart hammering in her chest. She stared at the graphs on the screen on her phone, willing them to change. When they didn't, she switched to her inbox, to find some comfort and reassurance there – messages from followers telling her how awesome or inspirational she was, perhaps, or a voice note from Zal checking in.

But with a crushing sense of disappointment, Barb realised there were no messages from Zal. And she had only one message from a follower. One! How quickly she had been forgotten, how speedily everyone had moved on.

Barb went to open the message – one was better than none, she supposed – feeling a strange mixture of sadness and self-loathing. She saw the handle. It was @OfficialO, the 'official' clearly an attempt to look more important than she was rather than anything *actually* official. Like putting a blue heart in your handle to make it look to the casual observer that you had a blue tick. She usually ignored messages like this because they normally only wanted something from you – to share some content they had done, for example, or to ask you for advice on how to build a successful social media profile – but the fact that it was the only one led her in.

@OfficialO: 'Hey Barb, I know this is going to seem weird given that you don't know me . . . but I feel like I know you from following you and I noticed that you haven't been online for five days and I just wanted to check all was OK with you? I love following you, your content gives me so much joy, and I wanted to let you know that. Come back soon, we miss you! xx'

The message was so kind that Barb thought she might cry. She clicked on @OfficialO's name, thinking she would follow her back as a measure of her gratitude, of her relief that a single human being out there actually cared about her wellbeing.

And it was then that she saw the one picture the account had posted.

As she looked at it, all the colours seemed to swirl around in front of her eyes as her brain tried to make sense of what she was looking at.

An identical photo to the one that Barb kept hidden under her pile behind her door: the photo of her mum sitting on the steps of the monument in the park, her hair as gold as the Buddha, smoking.

CHAPTER 14

If that morning Barb had felt like the Warriner Skeleton, now Barb felt like the Warriner Robot: blank, mechanical, getting on with things as she was supposed to, but without any knowledge of how or why she was doing them. It was as if her brain had shut down after being overwhelmed by what she had seen. Everything she thought she knew had been wiped from her brain in a single moment. She went about her day on autopilot, a machine with instructions but no particular feelings about them.

She had a shower. She brushed her teeth. She tried to blow dry what remained of her hair, feeling curiously detached from the patchy mess that greeted her in the mirror. She got dressed, selecting outfits from her wardrobe as if she had been preprogrammed to do so. She put on the hat that her aunt had thrown her earlier, and then she put on the most artificial of smiles, selected from a drawer in her brain, which she felt sure she was going to need if she was going to get through the rest of the day.

'What are you doing?' Sorcha shouted across the flat as she laid eyes on Barb.

'I'm putting my shoes on to go outside,' replied Barb in her most human voice.

'Outside?' Barb watched as Sorcha's nostrils flared with fury. 'You're planning on going OUTSIDE? Have you lost your mind as well as your hair?'

Barb's robot brain decided it was probably not the best time to tell her aunt that actually, she had lost her mind, around an hour and a half ago on receiving a message from a person who was supposed to be dead.

Instead, she nodded mutely and began undoing her shoes.

'You didn't think you were leaving the house with your hair like that, did you?' Sorcha shuddered as she said this. She didn't wait for a response. 'Good God, we are *not going anywhere* until we've sorted that mess out. Imagine if someone saw you! Imagine if the wind whipped up and your hat flew off and the whole of Battersea realised that you were going bald? Not on my watch, Barb. *Not on my watch!* You're staying in this tower block until you've got so much bloody hair you can throw it over the balcony and people can climb up it to visit us.' She took a breath and then started marching up and down the living room. 'You are not leaving this flat until you make Rapunzel look like The *effing* Rock!' Sorcha seemed particularly pleased with this analogy and let out one of her cackles.

Barb sat down on the sofa and waited for the tirade to end. When Sorcha finally stopped finding herself hilariously funny, she straightened up and cleared her throat. 'Juan's friend Extension Amy is coming to us,' explained Sorcha. 'She doesn't do house calls for just anyone, so be nice, OK?'

Robot Barb wondered when, exactly, she had been anything other than nice.

Just then, the buzzer went. Sorcha rearranged her features from angry headmistress in distress to happy hostess with the mostest. She went to the intercom and spoke into the phone. 'Amy! Come right up. If you don't mind taking the stairs . . . unfortunately the lift broke last night and the concierge is still working on fixing it!'

Robot Barb wondered for a moment what planet her aunt lived on.

Sorcha ran to the mirror and checked her face. She smoothed down her hair and applied some more lipstick, as if any of it mattered in the slightest. Then she positioned herself next to the door and waited for Amy to climb the stairs. 'Look *happy*!' she spat in Barb's direction. 'Look welcoming!'

There was a knock on the door and Sorcha opened it

while clapping her hands together in glee. 'Amy! Our saviour! Our heroine! Come in!'

Barb listened to her aunt's voice go up several octaves and was reminded of that awful day when they had visited Spark Enterprises, when all the artifice in the world could not have hidden how completely out of their depth they both were.

Amy walked through the door. A vision in leather trousers, a cropped leather jacket, and five-inch stilettos, not a hair out of place – and she hadn't broken into a sweat despite the climb she had just undertaken. She chewed some gum, surveyed the small flat, and then let her blown-up lips curl into something approaching pity. 'Cute place,' she said, not at all authentically. 'That walk is great exercise for the thighs, eh?'

If Barb had been human right then, she would have noted that Amy barely had any thighs to speak of – indeed, there didn't seem to be a shred of flesh on her body. Everything seemed . . . well, plastic, from her hair to her forehead to her lips to her pleather trousers.

'Can I get you something to drink?' asked Sorcha, ushering Amy to the armchair, the one Barb had never been allowed to sit on because of some unspoken rule that it was only for grown-ups. Or only for Sorcha.

Amy looked down at the armchair, and then used her acrylic nails to wipe invisible dirt from the cushions. Finally, she sat down and looked at Sorcha. 'I'd love a sparkling water,' she said with a smile as fake as the hair fanning perfectly across her shoulders.

Sorcha gave as good as she got and plastered on a rictus grin. 'Oh goodness, we're all out, I'm so sorry, the Ocado delivery isn't due until tomorrow!'

It would have amazed Barb, had Robot Barb not been sitting in her place, how, even now, in such desperate times, her aunt could still be bothered to pretend that they were anything other than people who drank tap water and shopped at the local Asda.

'Still?'

Amy winced. 'That's OK.'

'How about a tea?' suggested Sorcha desperately.

'Great idea, I'll have peppermint.'

Sorcha let out a shrill laugh. 'Unfortunately—'

'Don't tell me, you're out of peppermint tea?'

'Well yes, but I've got some PG Tips left?'

'I'm fine actually,' said Amy with a disdain that said she absolutely wasn't fine actually. She would clearly rather have been anywhere *but* this sad flat twelve floors up in the south London sky.

But really, Robot Barb thought, with a small flash of sudden feeling, *who could blame her?*

'Anyway, I'm not here for refreshments, am I?' asked Amy. 'I'm here because Juan is a good friend and I owe him a favour cos he used to colour my hair for free before I got extensions. And he tells me your daughter needs help.'

Sorcha coughed and Barb shut down completely. It was the only thing she could do to stop herself from standing up and screaming down the whole estate. She focused on her breathing – iiinnn through her nose, ooouuut through her mouth.

'Actually, I'm not her daughter. She's my guardian. But that's sort of by the by. It's very kind of you to come along and offer your help, because I really need it.' And then Barb sat up straight and removed her hat.

Sorcha winced. Amy gasped. Barb ploughed on regardless.

'As you can see, I am losing my hair. I have what I think is alopecia areata, and I know from research that it might progress to alopecia totalis, which would involve losing all the hair on my head. The worst-case scenario is alopecia universalis, which would involve losing all the hair on my body.' Barb paused and allowed both Sorcha and Amy to make the appropriate noises of horror that they clearly needed to make; a 'What?' from Sorcha and an 'Oooh' from Amy, as if Barb was telling her a particularly fascinating bedtime story.

Barb cleared her throat and continued her robot speech. 'I don't know if Juan mentioned, but I am a content creator on social media and the content I create is around my hair. It used to be really long and, I guess, lovely. It's the

213

only thing that anyone ever really noticed about me for as long as I can remember – in the park, in the supermarket, wherever we went, people stopped and mentioned how amazing my hair was.' Barb saw a strange look cross her aunt's face, but continued: 'And I always loved things like YouTube. With my friend Jess' – her voice broke a bit, and she coughed to gain composure – 'we used to dream of being social media stars. As I got a bit older, my aunt suggested I start a ShowReal account as a way for me to pay my way here in the flat and make a living. I left school last summer, and I've–' Just in time, Barb noticed her aunt's glare and corrected herself. '*We've* put everything into making this work and it's been quite successful, until now.' She put her hand to her head and felt its smoothness. 'Until this. Do you think you might be able to help?'

And then the strangest thing happened next. Amy stood up from the armchair, walked towards Barb, sat down on the sofa next to her, and hugged her. In fact, it was more than a hug. It was an *embrace*. She clutched Barb to her fake bosom and she didn't let go. Amy may have looked as fake as you got, but in that moment, Barb had never felt a physical embrace so genuine. It startled Barb to the point that she thought she might start crying, too.

'You poor, poor thing,' said Amy, stroking what remained of Barb's hair. 'You're just a child and you've been through all this pressure. No wonder your body is reacting in this way. You absolute love.'

Barb breathed in Amy's perfume and wondered for a moment if she could ask Amy to adopt her.

Then Amy moved out of the embrace, put her hands on Barb's shoulders, and smiled benignly at her. 'I'm so sorry for all you've been through.'

For a few moments Barb had forgotten about her aunt. Then Sorcha started up her loud cackling again, and the spell was broken. 'It's very sweet to see how concerned you are for Barb's wellbeing, but what I really want to know is, can you sort out her hair so she doesn't look like someone's gone mad with a men's beard trimmer? Because that's the only thing that is really going to make any of this better.'

Amy shook her head and let out a small, ever-so-slightly exasperated sigh. Barb looked at her and then at the cynical glare on her aunt's face, and she felt the jolts massing inside her stomach, threatening to upend her robot brain. But before they could, Amy began speaking very firmly. 'Let me tell you about hair extensions. They work great if you've got slightly thinning hair, if your hair grows slowly, or if you want longer hair for a bit but don't actually want to grow it. But they are a temporary thing. And they're not the answer for this condition. They pull on the scalp and could actually make it worse. You'd be much better off getting a wig and then focusing your attention on why her hair is falling out.'

Amy turned to Barb, a look of genuine concern on her face. 'Barb, I'm sorry you are being made to feel that the way you look is a problem. I think you're beautiful. But really, it doesn't matter what I think. You can have all the hair, all the lip fillers, all the boob jobs and all the collagen implanted in your cheeks that you might wish for, but none of it will matter if you don't have love in your heart. *For yourself*. Listen to me, Barb. I know I look all glamorous and put together, but it's just part of the job. It's simply a uniform that enables me to look the part while I'm doing my work. But I can't do the job and help clients feel good about themselves if I don't feel good about myself. If it's all for show.' She paused, looking frankly at Barb. 'So the way I am going to help you today is to tell you – forget about your hair and work on getting some love for yourself, feelings of worth and esteem, into that beautiful heart of yours. Then everything else will fall into place. But until you do that, this problem with your hair is only going to carry on or keep popping up in some different way.'

Barb felt a tear fall on to her cheek. She was vaguely aware that it belonged to her. Then the thought was disturbed by a screeching sound coming from the direction of her aunt. Barb gulped.

Sorcha looked as if she was going to spontaneously combust with rage. 'HOW DARE YOU?' her aunt screamed. 'You waltz in here looking like a Barbie doll and accuse US of being fake? The only real thing about you is the bile that just came out of your collagen-enhanced lips! How dare you presume to have a clue about us or tell us how to live our lives? I'm the ONLY person who has ever loved that girl. Everyone else upped and left it to me – her mum, her dad, her best friend . . . none of them gave a shit about Barb but me. I'm the only one who has stuck with her through thick and thin, and you come here and tell me that I don't love her? That *I'm* the one with the problem? NO. No, I won't take that! If it wasn't for me, she'd have ended up being taken into care. I've worked hard almost my whole adult life to bring this girl up, and I won't have some woman in a pair of fake leather trousers come in and tell me I've gone about it all wrong!'

'Sorcha!' exclaimed Barb, partly in protest at her language, partly in an attempt to calm things down. 'Forget about it. It doesn't matter. None of it matters.'

'Oh, but it does, Barb. It matters, all right. Because without your hair, you're nothing, and you know it.'

Barb crumpled on to the sofa, the robot finally fully gone from her brain. Amy shook her head in horror, opened her mouth to say something, then closed it, shook her head again and made her way towards the door. She paused before she got there. She clearly had one more thing she wanted to say.

'You know, maybe this girl's hair, or lack of it, isn't the

problem.' She opened the door and stepped out. 'Maybe, as her *guardian* – the person who is supposed to be protecting her – maybe your attitude towards her hair is the problem.' And then she closed the door behind her, the sound of its slam waking Barb out of a sixteen-year nightmare.

CHAPTER 15

The strangest thing was happening to Barb McDonnell, and it wasn't the fact that all her hair was falling out. In fact, the most peculiar thing was occurring *inside* her head, below the bald patches and thinning straggles of stringy hair that now made up her scalp.

It was as if the more she lost the hair on her head, the more she gained a sense of self inside it.

With each disappeared golden lock, she seemed to be discovering a previously unknown part of her character: a spunk, a sass, a solid idea of how she actually felt. Her hair had been her only defining characteristic for sixteen long years, and now, as it fell away, she was finally discovering what it had been hiding for so long.

The moment Amy had walked out of the door, Barb had well and truly shed her robot self. She got up from the sofa, marched to the kitchen, grabbed a box of Weetabix and some milk, and made her way to her bedroom, where she slammed the door with a satisfying loudness she had never made before.

Indeed, as the door flew towards the door frame, connecting with a loud THUNK, she realised she had never slammed anything in an adolescent huff in her entire life.

As the sound resonated in her room, the 'reach for the stars' poster fell to the floor with a clatter, and Barb started to laugh. She imagined her aunt's shocked face on the other side of the wall and a spurt of joy erupted inside her. She laughed a bit louder, as loud as any of the times Sorcha had cackled at her own lame jokes. Barb realised then that the slammed door was the tip of a very large iceberg of teenage things she had never done: she had never kissed anyone; never stayed out late and come home drunk, vomiting everywhere (she didn't think looking after her aunt in such a state counted for this); had never smoked; never shouted at Sorcha that she hated her life; never complained that everything was sooo unfair.

From the moment she was born, Barb had lived and breathed the belief that her very existence was at best a pain in the arse, at worst the reason for her mother's death. She had assumed that every single move she made was an annoyance to someone out there, be it Sorcha or Jess or an anonymous troll.

At that moment, a notification flashed up on her screen.

A new voice note from Zal. Her heart thumped as she pressed play.

@IAmZal: 'Excuse me, Little Miss Mysterious, but where you been? I thought we were friends and you're basically *ghosting me*? Man, we have to rectify that quickly. Message me. Laters.'

The tone in his voice was cheery, jokey. She wasn't an annoyance to *him*. She saw the message as a sign from the universe: she was so used to thinking of herself as the problem that it had never occurred to her that, actually, maybe she was the *solution*. And that maybe someone else was the problem.

Barb stomped round her room, letting out all the fury she supposed she should have let out a long time ago. Like, sixteen years ago. She was angry, confused, and terribly, terribly sad. A hot rage seemed to course through her, only to disappear suddenly, extinguished by a fast-flowing river of tears. She had no idea what was happening to her – just that, whatever it was, it needed to happen.

She needed to get it all out, whether Sorcha liked it or not.

For Barb's entire life, she had felt as if she was waiting for something. Until that strange day when she found the first patch.

She had never felt right. She had never felt like she belonged. Every time some stranger commented on the beauty of her hair, it hadn't made her feel happy or grateful – it had just made her feel self-conscious and awkward. For so many people, her aunt included, it seemed that physical beauty was the be all and end all. But it had driven Barb into herself, until she realised she had no real idea who she was. She existed to please other people, but when had she ever done anything that pleased her?

And then there was Zal. Physical beauty meant nothing to him, and he was the most content person she knew.

So now . . . now she was going to start living for herself. Not for her aunt. Not for people like Anna G. And most certainly not for an *algorithm*.

Barb started by pulling down the other framed posters on her wall. 'If opportunity doesn't knock, build the door' went first – opportunity had not knocked, and now she was going to build a door out of this bloody room if it was the last thing she did. She retched a little as she took down 'Life is not about waiting for the storm to pass, but learning to dance in the rain'. Not only was it unbelievably corny, it also reminded her that she had absolutely *no* idea what the weather was like outside, and nor had she done for some time now. She stamped on 'Shoot for the moon – if you miss you will land among the stars' and grinned widely as she watched the cheap plastic frame crack. Then she did the same with the others before removing the prints from the broken frames and ripping them to pieces.

She went to her phone and did not open her social media apps. Instead, she plugged her phone into her speakers, turned up the volume as high as it would go and pressed play.

Barb drew the blinds, she opened the window, and as 'Teenagers' by My Chemical Romance blasted out she jumped on the bed and screamed. She did not care who heard her – being heard was the whole point. She had lived in this oppressive bedroom her whole life, barely leaving, her world as tiny as the screen on her iPhone. Now she needed to make her world big. She needed to make her world *true*.

Over the blare of the music, Barb just about heard her aunt hammering on the wall. She ignored it. Barb was done letting her aunt make all the noise in this flat. In fact, she was done letting her aunt make noise on her behalf. She was done with being quiet and agreeable, with moulding herself into increasingly difficult positions to make other people happy.

Sorcha had asked Amy to help – and she had, though not in the way that Sorcha had intended. Barb had needed to hear those words come out of someone else's mouth, and once they had come tumbling out, the thing she had been trying to make sense of for so long had suddenly become clear. Sorcha was the difficult person, not Barb. If anything, Barb had bent over backwards to be accommodating to her aunt, to the point that she had been prepared to stab her best mate in the back and ruin the one proper friendship she had had since childhood.

Because, in truth, it was Sorcha who was to blame for Jess and Barb's falling out. Sorcha had never liked her niece hanging out with Jess, and she certainly hadn't liked the idea that Barb had come to her with that fateful day when everything had come to an end. They had been so excited about it, Jess and Barb. They had been planning it for years, really, ever since they first started watching those toy-unboxing videos when they were little kids. They were going to start a YouTube channel together. Finally, they were going to have a go at doing the thing they had always dreamed of. They had been cooking it up properly for months.

The plan was simple: it would be devoted to all things hair, with Jess styling Barb's locks into amazing creations that would wow their audience and win them hundreds of thousands – if not *millions* – of subscribers. They would shoot, edit and produce the content together. They would be a double act, an unstoppable force powered by years of friendship. People would watch their videos as much for their chat as for the hairstyles – they would provide hair tutorials that were both informative and entertaining.

Together, they had saved up for things like a tripod and a ring light. Jess had told her dad about it and he had been encouraging: he saw it as a great side project, a way to hone valuable skills outside school. Behind his back, Jess had rolled her eyes at his sweet naivety – the plan, of course, was to make this their everything, their life, their escape from the tedium of Queenstown Academy. They had done a few pilots, to practise, and they were ready to go live.

There had been just one thing standing in their way: given that they were under the age of seventeen, they needed Sorcha's permission, as well as Pete's, to set up a YouTube channel.

Jess had been confident that Sorcha would be fine with it. Barb, less so. She knew her aunt, after all, while Jess had only really witnessed her from a distance. 'You always say how much she loves social media,' Jess said one day as she plaited Barb's hair into a lavish braid. 'Also, she's hardly the most hands-on of guardians. Just tell her! What's the worst that could happen?'

So Barb had taken a deep breath, and the worst had happened.

Afterwards, Barb couldn't tell Jess the full truth of what Sorcha had said. She couldn't repeat the bile that had fallen so easily out of her aunt's mouth. How could she tell her best friend what her aunt thought? That, according to Sorcha, Jess was not a mate but a leech, hanging on to Barb's coat-tails (or her hair), trying to hitch a ride on Barb's talent. Barb couldn't tell Jess that Sorcha had other plans: plans for Barb to move on to ShowReal, not YouTube (YouTube, according to Sorcha, was old hat). She couldn't tell her friend that Sorcha said she would never, ever allow her to do a channel as long as it was with Jess.

'I've always said you're better than that girl,' spat Sorcha after Barb had cheerfully revealed their plan. 'I'm not going to stand by and watch her suck all your potential out for her own gain! You can play at being YouTube stars with her, but you're not doing it for real unless you go it alone. You don't need her. The only person you need behind you is *me!*'

Instead, Barb had knocked on Jess's door with tears in her eyes; when Jess opened the door she hadn't had to say anything at all.

'She said no, didn't she?' Jess gulped.

Barb nodded. 'We just have to wait a couple of years until we're old enough,' she said desperately, tears falling down her face. 'Then we don't need her permission.'

'I need some time alone, Barb,' she said. 'I need a bit of space, I think. I'll get in touch when I'm ready.'

Two weeks later, Barb uploaded her first video to the profile Sorcha had created. How to get the glossiest locks in town. A month later, she had already amassed five thousand followers . . . but she had lost the one person who really mattered to her, and that was Jess.

Barb was shocked out of the memory by hammering on her bedroom door, hammering so loud it had somehow cut through the music. Out of the corner of her eye, Barb saw it swing open.

'BARB!' screeched her aunt, a look of blind panic on her heavily made-up face. 'Turn that music down NOW!' When Barb made no motion to do that, Sorcha walked to the speakers and fiddled around with them until the noise disappeared.

Then Barb got down from her bed, walked over to her aunt, and grabbed the speakers from her hands. 'No,' she said, turning the volume back up. 'No. I will no longer be QUIET!'

It was as if Barb had slapped Sorcha in the face. Her jaw fell almost to the floor, where she saw the torn posters and the broken frames. 'You've gone insane!' she squawked over the music. 'Completely insane!'

But Barb was not going to let her aunt have the last word, not this time. 'No, Sorcha,' she said, pushing her towards the door and then out the other side of it. 'I've gone sane, actually. For the first time in my life, I feel completely and utterly sane.' Then she slammed the door again, and went back to dancing on her silly, gifted bed, like the silly, gifted teenager she was always meant to be.

Later, when she had got some of it out of her system, a calm fell over Barb. She picked up the posters and the frames and took them to the bin in the kitchen.

Sorcha buzzed around her like a fly as she made herself a massive glass of orange squash. 'Have you taken your vitamins?' she asked, again and again and again.

Barb ignored her, again and again and again. She went back to her room instead to make her bed, but her aunt followed her.

'Barb, darling.' Sorcha pulled her mouth into a rictus smile. 'I know you're upset but I really need to talk to you.'

Barb silently straightened the duvet and plumped up the pillows, trying to do her best to pretend that her aunt was not there. 'I know that hair-extension lady was upsetting and I'm sorry I invited her in here. It was thoughtless of me. I thought perhaps we could go and see a homeopath. Like a doctor, but one who works with herbs rather than all that toxic medicine. I've looked up a really good one and been in touch with them and they would love to see you in return for a bit of content. I think it could really help with the hair loss, in a way that's not as intrusive as that Amy lady. She was just so—'

'Stop.' Barb turned towards her aunt and stared her

down. 'Please just stop. I don't want to see a witch doctor—'

'A HOMEOPATH!'

'A whatever.' Barb was calm, collected, speaking confidently. 'I don't want to see a homeopath or a hair-extension specialist or anyone right now. And the person I don't want to see the most, I'm afraid, is you. Because you don't get it, do you? You don't get that this doesn't work for me. That it's not working for you, either. I'm tired of this. Really tired. I want to start actually living my life, outside this stifling flat. I want to live in the real world, not this made-up digital one.'

She marched over to the pile of laundry in the corner and rummaged for the photograph of her mother, the one by the gold Buddha. She held it up, right in Sorcha's face. 'But mostly I want to know the truth.'

It was Sorcha's turn to run away. Her face went white, and then she backed out of the door, as if her niece was some sort of monster. Barb heard her scramble for the fake Gucci bag, for her phone, for her keys, and then watched as she headed out of the flat, the front door slamming almost as loudly as Barb's bedroom door had done earlier. Barb was left alone with the photo and her thoughts, and the knowledge that there was something she needed to do.

She needed to speak to Jess.

CHAPTER 16

When Barb stepped outside on to the walkway that went past their front door that evening, she realised that the seasons had changed. The last time she had been out of the flat, she was certain that it was autumn, or maybe winter even. It had been dark and it had been cold enough that she had initially noticed the air on her skin in that ridiculous vintage dress. Now, though, it was still light and there was the delicious smell of spring in the air. Barb could even hear birds singing over the sounds of the traffic.

She breathed in deeply and shivered despite the warmth. It was more a shiver of recognition than of coldness: the recognition that she had no more time to waste. Too much of her life had passed inside her bedroom, staring at her phone. She stared down at the estate, noticing that children were actually playing on the swings. She smiled to herself. It felt like a good omen.

It was warm – warm enough that she felt the need to return briefly to the flat to dump her coat. But she kept on the hat. She realised she had completely come to terms with the state of her scalp, but she wasn't sure the same could be said for someone who hadn't seen it yet, and she thought that knocking on Jess's door would probably be enough of a shock for her former friend without also adding in the fact of her almost-baldness.

Barb couldn't be sure that Jess was in but she had to at least try and speak to her, and going around to hers was the only way she knew how to start: she had long ago been blocked by Jess on WhatsApp, and anyway, she didn't think she could say what she needed to via the cold, stark medium of a screen. It was the kind of thing that needed to be said face to face even if it was going to be incredibly painful to do so.

Barb had told herself this simple truth: she had felt enough pain recently to last a lifetime, and so she was well equipped to do this, however it turned out.

She walked down the stairs, putting fearful thoughts of Serena out of her mind. She ignored the glares of neighbours, who were unused to seeing her anywhere other than online.

She approached Jess's floor thinking of Zal: kind, lovely Zal, and how perhaps *this* was her version of the #WhatICouldntSee challenge. She tried to remember how

231

he made her feel: that with him behind her she could do anything. Barb stopped one step above Jess's floor, reached into her pocket and pulled out her phone. Hands shaking, she voice-noted Zal back. 'I just wanted to get in touch with you to apologise for going quiet on you. Some stuff has been going on and I should be sharing it with you, not holding it back from you. And I will do. I just have one more thing to do, then I'll be right back. Miss you.'

It was time.

Looking along the walkway, she could see that the kitchen lights were on in Jess's flat and that a pair of her wedges had been left outside the door, presumably kicked off after the long slog up the stairs. Barb felt a flutter in her chest, but she did not feel any jolts. She was calm, so calm – as calm as she had been when she first discovered that alopecia patch.

She approached the flat, knowing that there was no turning back: not from Jess's front door, and not from this moment of realisation that she needed to escape Sorcha and all that she stood for.

With all the strength inside her, Barb went to knock. But before her knuckles could touch the wooden frame of Jess's front door, it swung open – revealing the thunderous face of her former friend.

* * *

'What the hell do you want?' said Jess, shaking her head in disgust. She didn't even seem to notice the strange hat on Barb's head. Instead, she stood there, a glare on her so harsh that Barb thought it might have the power to dislodge what remained of her hair. But she breathed through the glare and all the voices inside her that urged her to bolt back up the stairs to the flat.

And still the jolts did not come.

'I want to apologise,' Barb replied, quickly.

'You're lucky I even opened the door. Serena saw you out her window coming down the stairs and warned me. How *dare* you think you can just come here out of the blue, as if it's the most normal thing in the bloody world?'

'I, I . . .' Barb was stammering, but she knew she had to keep it together. 'I've got a lot to say sorry for, I know that. I'm sorry I went behind your back with my own social media channel. I'm sorry I let all its glitz distract me from what really matters.' Barb noticed that Jess's expression was changing a little – becoming more confused if anything. 'I miss you. I miss us.' Barb put her hand firmly on her thumping heart. 'I was wrong, listening to my aunt. I've seen her for what she really is. I should never have listened to her over you and followed our social-media dream alone. My life is horrible without you in it. I've known it for ages, but I've also found something out that has made me realise I needed to come down here and apologise.'

233

'And what could that be?' Jess tried to spit the words out, but she couldn't quite muster the required hostility.

'Sorcha's been lying to me. About my mum. I think . . .' Barb breathed in deeply. 'I think she's alive.'

She couldn't believe she'd finally said it. That the words had come out of her mouth, making it real. Jess really looked at Barb then. Her eyes shifted from quizzical to shocked. She gulped back something, and then she stepped forward towards her old friend. 'You mean you didn't know? All this time, you didn't know?' Her eyes narrowed, expressing something close to horror, and suddenly it was Barb who was thrown into confusion. 'You'd better come in.'

It was surreal, being back inside Jess's flat. For years she had been dreaming of lofty things like social media stardom, but for the last few months all she had dreamed of was this: standing in Jess's home again, hanging out with her oldest mate. It was exactly as Barb remembered it: she could see, through Jess's bedroom door, that she definitely *did* still have the Chelsea FC bedspread and the dreamcatcher hanging overhead.

Barb stood and surveyed this place of safety, realising how profoundly unsafe she had felt since she had last been inside it. She turned around to Jess, her head spinning. It was all too much: being outside her flat for the first time in for ever; hearing that Jess knew about her mum; realising that there was so much more to the story of her life than she had ever known.

'You need to sit down,' said Jess, motioning towards a sofa. 'You're like the walking, talking version of someone who has *actually* seen a ghost.'

Barb didn't have the power of speech inside her so she couldn't reply that, actually, that was *exactly* what she had seen: the ghostly picture of her mother on social media attached to an account that had been alive enough to send her a message. Instead, Barb did as she was told and fell back on to the sofa. She felt the tears come spilling out of her. She was sobbing, properly sobbing, as she had never done before.

'I can't believe you didn't know all this time,' said Jess, walking to the kitchen to get her a glass of water.

Barb took it gratefully, hands shaking. She still couldn't speak so she let Jess do all the talking. 'I'm trying to get this straight in my head, so excuse me if it comes out all wrong, but you thought I wasn't talking to you because you set up a social media profile *without* me?'

Barb looked up from the cup and nodded.

'You actually thought that I would drop years of friendship because of YouTube?' Jess shook her head and dropped to the sofa next to Barb. 'And you really, genuinely had no idea that your mum's alive? You hadn't been lying to me?'

'No – what are you talking about?' Barb managed through numb, trembling lips as she tried to piece together what was happening.

Finally Barb found the words. 'You said you needed space to clear your head and then I didn't hear from you, so of course I thought it was about that.' The words made Barb start to sob again and she had to wait to let it pass. 'Then Sorcha encouraged me to start my own feed and I just assumed you hated me because I'd gone behind your back and done it without you.'

Jess stood up and started pacing the room. 'Jesus, Barb,' she exclaimed. 'As if I would drop years of friendship because of *that*.' She rolled her eyes in that familiar Jess way, and it made Barb's heart swell with the sense that even though everything was very, very wrong, it was going to be all right. 'Barb McDonnell! Please, never, ever, *ever* assume that we're all as shallow as your bloody aunt. The reason I was disappointed about the YouTube thing was because it was something we could do together. But it's not the reason I've been quiet on you. The reason I've done that is because all this time I thought you were lying to me. I thought you *knew* that your mum was alive. I thought that all these years you'd been spinning me some yarn, leading me on over the fact I don't, well, you know . . . my mum's not around any more. I thought you were responsible for the deception of the bloody *century*.'

She sat back down next to Barb and blew out an enormous breath of air.

Barb tried to form a response but it refused to come. Her head felt it contained just a complete blur of tears and confusion.

'After you told me that Sorcha had said no to the channel, I was upset, of course I was. I'm human, right?' Jess shrugged. 'I told my dad, who was like, "It's for the best, the McDonnells are the weirdest family the Warriner Estate has ever seen, and that's saying something." When I asked him what he was talking about, he completely clammed up and then I *knew* he was keeping something from me.'

Barb thought about that moment when Pete had asked her about her mum, when she had sensed something move in his eyes. It was all falling into place.

'I was really upset and eventually I got it out of him: he told me that your mum wasn't dead as you'd always said; that she was alive and the last he'd heard was that she was trying to dry out the same way my mum was: in a detox clinic. He'd just assumed you said she'd died because you were in denial or not very well. He'd taken pity on you and then he could hardly tell me, as a little kid, the truth. He thought you were lying because you were so ashamed of what had really happened: that your mum had given you up because she was a junkie.'

Barb gasped, her face frozen, the blood draining from it. And she could see by the look on Jess's face that Jess now completely believed that Barb had not been lying to her.

Jess's phone vibrated and she killed the call. 'I can deal with Serena later.'

Barb flinched at the mention of Serena's name and Jess looked at her.

'Look, Barb. I know we've not exactly been kind to you recently but, Jesus, I thought that all my life you'd been bullshitting me. I was completely and utterly sideswiped. I couldn't work out why you hadn't just been honest with me, given that I of all people know *exactly* what it's like to be abandoned by a parent who loves getting wasted more than they love their own child.'

Barb felt the words go through her like a knife and collapsed in on herself. Jess reached for Barb and clutched her to her, and Barb knew it was her way of trying to comfort her as best, and as genuinely, as she could.

And it was then that Jess apparently noticed Barb was wearing a woollen hat over her glorious hair. 'Babes, I know this is probably going to sound a bit beside the point,' Jess said, looking at Barb as she held her close, 'but why the hell are you wearing a beanie hat in this weather?'

It was a day of revelations, that was for sure. Barb was completely overwhelmed with the news that her mother was still alive, that everyone but her knew she was still alive and that she was a drug addict . . . and so she was almost grateful for the distraction that her alopecia provided.

She sat up and whipped off the hat, revealing her ruined scalp in all its incredible weirdness.

Jess's head jolted up and she made a strange 'oh' sound. 'Did Sorcha do that?'

Barb actually laughed at the thought that her aunt would do anything to sabotage her precious hair – the only thing about her that Sorcha cared for.

'No.' She sniffed, wiping her nose. 'It's been falling out. It's called alopecia. This is all I've got left. At this rate, it won't be long before it's all gone.'

At that moment the front door swung open and Jess's dad, Pete, walked in. 'My goodness!' he exclaimed, dropping a bag of shopping to the floor, a head of broccoli rolling on to the carpet.

There was so much shock in the room that they could probably have fired the national grid, just the three of them.

'What the—'

'Dad,' Jess said, cutting in. 'Barb didn't know that her mum was alive. All this time she didn't know.'

'Never mind about that for now,' said Pete, whose jaw had followed the shopping bag to the floor. 'What's happened to your hair, Barb? Are you OK?'

'I'm fine,' said Barb, and she was surprised to find she

genuinely meant it. 'I'm actually probably in the best place I've been my whole entire life, despite how I look.'

'Our sofa is the best place you've been in your whole entire life?' said Jess with a mischievous smile. 'And you went to Catrina's make-up launch, so that's *quite* the compliment.'

Barb started laughing, and then realised what Jess had just said. 'You knew I went to that?' She was surprised, astounded, even.

'Of course I knew,' said Jess, looking at Barb as if she had lost her mind and not just her hair. 'I may not have been talking to you but do you think I haven't been checking your profile?' She shook her head and laughed.

Barb laughed back and then threw her arms around her oldest friend. The fact that Jess had been looking at her page all this time was a small thing, but somehow, amongst all the chaos of her life, it meant the absolute world.

CHAPTER 17

It seemed logical after that, that Barb should come and stay with Jess and her dad. She could hardly go back to the flat on the twelfth floor after everything she had just learnt, which was pretty mind-blowing: she had not killed her mum; her mum had not, actually, been killed at all and was alive and presumably well enough to be sending her messages on social media; she lived with a liar; Jess hadn't been ignoring her because of the YouTube stuff at all.

That evening Pete had made the girls the same dinner he created on all those old play dates: fish fingers, potato waffles, and the broccoli that had rolled out on to the carpet. Plus lashings and lashings of ketchup.

As they wolfed down their dinner, he had told Barb everything he knew: 'Your mums weren't friends before they got pregnant with you,' he explained to the girls.

'Everyone called them trouble. But really they were just in a lot of pain from their own upbringings, like so many people, and booze and drugs were the only ways they knew how to escape it. I was hardly an innocent myself, you know.' He raised his eyebrows and Jess made a mock-retching sound. 'Don't worry, sweetheart. I was never into it like they were. I could be a bit out there but I was always the tame one. Mr Responsible they used to call me.'

Pete paused for a moment and got up to put more waffles in the toaster. 'Then your dad died of an overdose, Barb. I didn't really know him well, but he seemed like a nice man, Stuart.' Barb could not believe that she was hearing her father's name for the first time in her life. 'He was just unlucky, really. He was at home alone. He was always alone whenever he was at home – his parents were . . . neglectful. They didn't even come to the funeral. It gave us all a shock, I can tell you. And then pretty quickly after that both Orla and your mum, Jess, found out that they were pregnant with you two. That was how they became friends. We had all these plans, you know. Your mums were going to share childcare and get jobs and start their lives properly.' He stared at the toaster and shook his head. 'They really, really thought that getting pregnant was the end of their wild days. We were so naive, so young, we really thought that you girls were going to do for them what rehab does for everybody else. It genuinely never occurred to any of us

242

that they'd pick right up where they left off.' The toaster popped, and Pete got up and put the waffles on a plate, before placing them in the middle of the table and sitting back down.

Barb was practising the deep breathing – iiinnn through her nose and outtttttt through her mouth – because otherwise she was going to faint.

Pete carried on. 'You were born, what, a month apart? You first, Barb. God, all that hair!' He chuckled. 'Quite the talking point. Orla was so bloody in love with you, you know.'

Barb tried to do the in and out breathing.

'Your mum, too, sweetheart, when you were born.' He looked at Jess, who clenched her jaw and scowled. She had clearly heard this before but seen no actual evidence of it so far. 'We were all smitten. I know it might seem really hard to understand that now, but if I've learnt anything through this whole experience, it's that love doesn't make the slightest goddamn difference to addiction. It will tear its claws through it, rip love apart. You think, "How can they not stop for the children?" But it doesn't work like that. It doesn't work like that.'

Barb thought she saw his eyes glistening. Then Pete closed his eyes and put his hands over his face. Barb closed hers too and tried not to cry. She felt Jess's hand make its way to hers, and held it tight.

'I remember when it happened so clearly. Watching your mums getting ready here. You were only a couple of months old and they were having a well-earned night out to The Secret Garden. They deserved it, right? They needed to let off steam, I thought. I was looking after you, Jess, and Sorcha was babysitting for you, Barb. Did you know she lived in east London then? She had this career and a boyfriend and a flat and she doted on you, too.' He sighed. 'She came over to babysit you that night, and she never left.'

Barb felt the tears prick her eyes and decided to let them come.

'They were missing for three days. We were out of our minds with worry but we knew, really, what had happened. They'd ended up on a bender they couldn't get off. They said they'd straighten out, that it was a one off, that they were still so young and they couldn't just be expected to suddenly leave all their wild ways behind them. But it just escalated, you know?'

Jess looked furious: she clearly didn't know, or care, for that matter. 'It was just out of control. So Sorcha and I decided to intervene properly before social services did, just until they sorted themselves out.'

'But they never did, did they?' Jess spat.

'No,' said Pete, sadly. 'No, certainly not Mum, Jess. I don't know about Orla. Sorcha didn't really want anything

244

to do with us once she had moved in properly. She wanted to take you to east London but she knew that would be complicated – it would alert the authorities, and anyway, her boyfriend was having nothing to do with it, and he was out of there when he realised she was actually serious about giving everything up to look after you. She wanted to start afresh, I think.' He looked at Barb now. 'I always assumed she'd told you and that she was just offish because . . . well, because it's hard isn't it? She had to give up everything, really, because of her sister's choices.'

For a moment, just a moment, Barb felt something like sympathy for her aunt. But her feelings were all over the place, and it was quickly swallowed up by her hunger to hear more.

'She couldn't stop you becoming friends at nursery, or later at school, but she certainly tried. That was the only time she ever spoke to me, actually – asking me to stop inviting you for play dates. But what was I to do? Jess only wanted to hang out with you. So Sorcha did her best not to interact with me, or Jess for that matter, even though she was only a kid. I guess you know that much, Barb.'

Barb nodded blankly. 'I always wondered why she was so against our friendship, why she never invited Jess to ours. Why she never wanted me to have a life outside the flat. God, she must have been so bloody glad when we stopped talking. I thought it was a bit crap that she was so happy when I was so miserable. And now I know why she was so over the moon about me leaving school, about me pursuing my own social media. Jesus.'

'I'm sorry I didn't talk more to you about it, Jess,' Pete continued. This was clearly difficult for him too. 'I just thought it was for the best. You both seemed completely caught up in your world of childish make-believe. And I really, genuinely assumed you were in denial, Barb. I thought it was some strange psychological coping mechanism that kids might employ to get through bad experiences. It wasn't as if I could talk to your aunt about it. She would turn and walk away with a scowl on her face whenever I went near her.' He shook his head. 'I'm just sorry I didn't intervene. That I didn't try and talk to you. Maybe I could have stopped it from getting to this point.' He motioned at Barb, whose eyes were streaming freely now. 'I'm so sorry. You poor, poor thing. You poor, poor things.'

That night Jess insisted that Barb sleep in her bed while she laid out a sleeping bag on the floor below her. 'You look knackered, Barb,' she said softly when Barb protested. 'You need to be looked after for once in your life and I'm going to do that. So comfortable bed it is.'

The window was cracked open, the dreamcatcher twinkling in the breeze. As they got ready for bed – Jess sorting her friend out with an oversized T-shirt – Barb realised she hadn't looked at her phone for hours. Without even *thinking* about it. She had switched it off after she left Zal a voice note before she had come down to Jess's flat, not wanting any distractions, and now she pulled it out of her pocket and watched as it flashed back into life.

Notifications started filling her screen: alerts about new content on ShowReal, followed by a series of increasingly frenzied WhatsApps from her aunt.

She sighed, deciding to look at those first.

Sorcha: Barb, I can explain everything, OK. Just please turn on your phone.

Sorcha: I think you've got the wrong end of the stick. The least you can do is hear me out.

Sorcha: BARB MCDONNELL, WHERE THE HELL ARE YOU? I'M WORRIED OUT OF MY BLOODY MIND.

Sorcha: Where have you gone? If you've gone to see that bloody Anna G I will be absolutely FUMING.

Sorcha: Listen, Barb, I'm sorry. I'm not thinking straight. Just please, please tell me where you are and I can make all of this right.

Sorcha: It's not what it looks like, it really isn't.

Sorcha: Please, Barb?

Barb ignored the messages and instead popped in her earphones to listen to the reply that Zal had sent.

@IAmZal: 'My God, you really are Miss Mystery. OK. You do what you got to do, and I'll be waiting for you when you're ready.'

Barb smiled, before slumping down on to the bed and letting out a sigh loud enough for Jess to comment on it.

'You OK?' she asked, flopping down beside her.

'You know, I'm not OK,' said Barb, emphatically. 'I'm really not. My whole life is a lie it turns out. My hair is almost gone.' She picked up a straggly bit. 'My hair, the only thing about me that has ever meant anything at all.'

'It's no—'

Barb cut Jess off. 'You said so yourself. You said I'm nothing without my hair. And you know, you were right at the time. I *was* nothing without my hair. My hair was all I had. I didn't have the truth. I didn't have the full story of who I really was. And so I *was* nothing without my hair. But now I know there was so much more there. And I only know that because I lost it. If it hadn't started falling out I would never have ended up finding any of this out. So no, I'm not OK. That's the truth. I'm being honest for once in my life. I'm an absolute mess. I'm in shock. I feel sick. I feel angry. But you know what, Jess?' Barb shifted and turned to look at her friend. 'I also feel overjoyed. Because even after all that, I'm still a hell of a lot better than I've ever been. Because now I know.'

And that was what she messaged her aunt. Those two words. 'I know'.

Sorcha could read into them what she wanted: she could live a life not knowing, for a little bit, what her niece meant, just as Barb had done for almost seventeen years.

And then she switched off her phone again. For there was nothing on it that could be more important than the moment she was living in right then.

As they got ready for bed, Barb realised that she was almost seventeen and she was on her first proper sleepover with a mate.

Those nights at the Real Res absolutely didn't count, given how her 'friendship' with Catrina had turned out.

As she got under the Chelsea FC bedspread she had thought about so much in the last year, she mentioned this to Jess, who was disappearing into her sleeping bag on the floor. 'Can you believe, Jess, that I haven't left my flat for months and months until today?'

Jess looked up and smiled sadly at her friend. 'I can, Barb. I really can. Sometimes, when I looked at your social media, I wondered if you ever did anything but film hair content in your bedroom. But let me tell you,' she said, reaching up to the bedside lamp and turning it off, 'this is just the beginning. There's a whole load of firsts out there for you to experience. A whole *world*.'

Quietly, in the darkness, Barb both smiled and sobbed at the same time.

CHAPTER 18

When Barb came to the next day, she felt like someone brought back to life after years in a coma. Her eyes flicked open suddenly and an icy panic gripped her stomach as the room around her came into focus. Where was she? Why were there no posters bearing crappy inspirational quotes on the wall, and why was the bed covered in a football team's branding?

And then she remembered. Jess. Pete. Her mum. Her aunt. Her *life*.

She peered over the side of the bed but Jess wasn't there – she had rolled up the sleeping bag and left it in the corner. Outside, Barb could hear the comforting clanking of pots and pans, the deliciously reassuring smell of eggs frying.

Barb rolled over and felt for her phone on the bedside table, and then propped herself up in the bed and stared at its dead black screen as she plucked up the courage to turn it on. It seemed silly, after all she had been through in the last twenty-four hours, to be scared of a tiny electronic device. But it wasn't so much the phone itself that scared Barb, more what was contained inside it. Abusive messages from Sorcha? Almost certainly. More information about her supposedly dead mum? That was always a possibility. All remaining evidence of the pathetic career she had carved out for herself in lieu of any actual GCSEs or A Levels? And yet the state of @letdownyourhair seemed the least trifling of her worries after everything that had come to light.

She turned on the phone, saw that it was almost midday and that she had slept for nearly twelve hours, and then braced herself for the barrage of messages she was about to receive from her aunt.

But only one came. She read it, her stomach rumbling.

Sorcha: Oh Barb, I'm so bloody sorry. I never meant for this to happen, for it to end up like this. It just sort of . . . got out of control in my immense fear at what was happening to your mum. But anything I say over WhatsApp is going to sound pathetic. And I know you're going to be angry, you have every right to be, so I'm not going to ask you for a chance to explain. I'm just going to let you know that when you are ready, I am here. And that I love you, even if it seems like the opposite is true.

Barb closed the message. Her aunt had never said the words 'I love you' before. It was, in a way, all Barb had ever

252

wanted: the knowledge that Sorcha actually cared about her. But she couldn't let it sway her. She hardened her heart. She needed to protect herself.

She opened her social media and scrolled past her interactions with Zal to the original message from @OfficialO.

Another one had been sent in the early hours of the morning. *Probably when she was off her head*, Barb thought spikily.

@OfficialO: 'I owe you an explanation. I owe you the truth. I'm so sorry. We're so sorry.'

One line in her inbox, as if that was all she deserved after everything. How fucking *dare* they? How dare they keep this from her. All this time Barb had felt like she was responsible for the death of her mother. How could they have lived through this deception, keeping Barb's world so small to cover up their lies? She thought she might scream the whole estate down, the whole world down, when suddenly a notification popped on to her screen.

Message @IAmZal.

He was always there, just when she needed him most. Even if he didn't *know* he was there, as he had been for her yesterday when she took the journey down the stairs to Jess's flat. She swiped out of the message from her mum – she felt the word sour in her stomach – and went to see what Zal had sent. It felt like an age since they had last spoken, in which time Zal had probably gained another million followers and been invited for tea with Barack Obama.

@IAmZal: 'STRANGER! You're online! I have been checking on you for ages now and you are never, ever active. There's no updates on your feeds, NOTHING. And now I sound like a stalker again. But I just wanted you to know I am thinking about you.'

Barb felt herself soften at the sound of his voice. She began recording a reply, desperate for interaction with him.

@letdownyourhair: 'Zal, you don't know how glad I have been to hear your voice. It's exactly what I need after the weeks I've had. I've got a lot to tell you about, so much so I'm not even sure it will fit in all the voice notes in the world. You could say I've had my own moment worthy of the #WhatICouldntSee hashtag.'

@IAmZal: 'Well, if it won't fit in a voice note, how about we meet up? IN REAL LIFE, LOL. There's so much we need to discuss. Like, did you see that Pixie has got sober, unfollowed Catrina and all the Spark Enterprises lot, and dumped Anna G as manager? GO PIXIE!'

@letdownyourhair: 'Well if Pixie is brave enough to do all of that, then I'm sure I can be brave enough to leave the estate and meet you face to face again.'

Barb put the phone down on the bedside table and allowed herself a moment to cheer for Pixie. For getting sober, as her mother had clearly failed to do, and for having the guts to break away from the toxic grip of Anna G. Then she remembered that *she* had also had some guts recently, and thought that maybe she should give herself the pat on the back she was always so ready to dish out to others but reluctant to give herself.

She had achieved more than she thought since leaving school. It had nothing to do with social-media engagement or money-making through brand partnerships. It couldn't be measured on ShowReal. But it was there and it was just as real . . . and it was worth more than all the ads or gifted tat in the world.

The bedroom door suddenly opened and Jess walked in brandishing a bowl of Weetabix on a tray. 'Breakfast in bed for Barb!' she trilled, walking over and placing the tray down on the bedside table. 'Welcome to the first day of the rest of your life!'

Barb smiled at the spread Jess had laid on for her. Weetabix, tea and fresh orange juice. 'That's so thoughtful,' she said, feeling almost moved to tears by this simple gesture.

Jess laughed. 'Has nobody ever made you a bowl of Weetabix before?'

Barb cast her mind back and realised that, no, nobody ever had.

Then Jess's voice softened. 'I've got lots to make up for. As does Serena.'

Barb had started spooning the mushy cereal into her

mouth, but at the mention of Serena's name she stopped, her stomach flipping in fear.

'You don't need to dive back under the duvet and quiver in terror,' said Jess, sensing the change in mood. 'I know that we both behaved like total cows, but we thought you were lying about your mum. I know that doesn't excuse the . . .' – Jess lost her words for a second – 'the moment I pulled your hair. That was bloody awful of me and I'm so sorry that I did it. It's not something I'm proud of at all, and I guess I was just in a dark place back then. I was super angry at you. I shouldn't have done it, but I'm glad I have a chance to apologise today. And I've spoken to Serena. I hope you don't mind, but I told her everything. About your mum and about your . . .' – Jess touched Barb's almost-bare scalp tenderly – 'about what has happened to your hair. Anyway, we're going to make it up to you.' She sat back and grinned at her friend. 'We need to get you off this bloody estate for a bit of fun. So how about a girls' evening at The Secret Garden tonight? Just the three of us.'

Barb's mouth formed a perfect O of horror and surprise. 'You want me to go on a girls' night out with *Serena*?'

Jess put on her most convincingly smiley face, similar to the one she had used when pretending on screen to be overjoyed at the knitted toilet-roll holder. 'Look, I know that you and Serena haven't exactly got off to the best start, but she's actually really kind when you get to know her.

When she lets you in. But Barb, it'll always be you and me. You know that, right? And you can always never speak to her again if you don't like her.'

'OK, two things,' said Barb, when she had finally got over the twin surprise of breakfast in bed *and* a social invitation from Serena. 'Firstly, The Secret Garden is not exactly getting me off the estate . . .'

Jess smiled. 'Sure, I know, but I thought it was a start. You know, ease you off gently and all that. And secondly?'

'Secondly,' said Barb, twirling her spoon in her bowl. 'I want to bring a friend too. My mate Zal.'

And now it was Jess's turn to be surprised.

The Secret Garden wasn't as glamorous as Barb had imagined it. In her mind, alone in her bedroom, it was a temple of hedonism where all the coolest people went. It had flashing lights, intimate corners, that kind of thing. In reality, it was a pub. A bog-standard pub just like the Queen Vic in *EastEnders*.

Barb hadn't been in any pubs in her life but she knew, the instant she walked in, that this one wasn't anything special. And the 'secret' garden in question that it took its name from? It was a patio out the back with a couple of broken tables and chairs that threatened to be strangled by weeds. *They could at least hang some fairy lights*, Barb thought.

Still, she wasn't complaining. It wasn't her bedroom or the flat, and that fact alone made it as exciting as a trip to the Ritz. It was a new place, some different scenery to absorb after all that time looking at the same four walls. And she told herself she didn't need to be embarrassed about bringing Zal here – he was the most grounded person she had met during this whole social media mess; she imagined he'd be happy hanging out on a park bench as long as the conversation was good.

She was more nervous about seeing Serena. But Barb knew she needed to at least give her a chance, even if she had to do it through gritted teeth.

Jess had shared her wardrobe with Barb for the evening ahead. Sure, Barb had a cupboard full of OKHUN's most plastic creations a few floors above, but she wasn't heading back there in a hurry and it wasn't as if she liked any of it anyway. She'd borrowed a pair of jeans, a T-shirt, and kept the beanie on as a sort of protection.

Together they had made their way to The Secret Garden, each tiny step down the stairs a move towards freedom. Barb felt something inside her, but it wasn't jolts. It was butterflies. As she approached The Secret Garden, she had tried to keep from her mind the memory of the last time she had been here: falling flat on her arse in front of Jess and Serena before that fateful night at the Shard. Now, though, there was no danger of doing that given that she was wearing her Fila trainers and she was excited, not scared.

She watched as an Uber pulled up outside the pub, and Zal got out. Barb ran towards him, brushing aside any notions of how uncool she was being.

'Zal!' she said, waiting for him to acknowledge that he knew she was there. 'It's me, Barb!'

She watched his mouth turn into a wide grin and then threw her arms around him.

'Barb!' He smiled. 'As I live and breathe, it's actually you in flesh and blood rather than on voice note.'

'This is my mate Jess,' Barb said, motioning towards her old friend before realising he couldn't see her do that. She laughed at herself as Jess stood there, grinning blankly, unsure what to do – when meeting a social-media star she was *obsessed* with.

'It's OK, Jess.' Barb smiled. 'You can shake his hand, you know!'

'Yeah,' said Zal. 'I won't bite it off or anything. In fact, why don't you give me a hug? Hand shaking is kind of awkward.'

Unbelieving, Jess put her arms around Zal and let out a little shriek. 'Sorry,' she said, pulling away. 'You probably hear this all the time but I just love what you do.' She waved her hands around in excitement.

'Right, calm yourself, Jess. Shall we go in?' Zal hooked

his left arm into Barb's and his right into Jess's. Then they walked through the door of The Secret Garden pub.

Inside, Serena was sitting alone at a table eating a packet of prawn cocktail crisps. A look of astonishment crossed her face when she saw Jess and Barb with Zal.

Barb guided Zal to a seat next to Serena and did the introductions. She waved politely at Serena, who mouthed the words 'I'm sorry' at her. Barb didn't respond. She focused instead on the prawn cocktail crisps, which she suddenly had an overwhelming need to devour.

'Right!' The fact that she had negotiated this moment with Serena without getting a jolt had given her a rush of energy. 'I'm going to get crisps!'

'Well,' Barb said, opening her bag of Skips when she had returned to their table. 'This is weird.' She was sitting in a pub, with friends, for the first time in her life.

'No,' said Zal, 'this is normal. What's weird is that you don't get out enough. Right, girls? Why haven't you forced her out before this?' He motioned in Jess and Serena's direction and they shifted awkwardly in their seats.

'So,' said Jess, 'we're here because Barb has had a bit of a few days . . .'

'I've had a bit of a life, actually,' Barb interrupted.

'Well, yes, a bit of a life,' acknowledged Jess, 'but then haven't we all?'

Quietly, the table nodded.

'What's been going on?' asked Zal. 'You've got me here – are you going to tell me why you've been so quiet?'

'I'll tell you,' said Serena with a mournful look on her face, as if explaining for Barb might make up for all the bullying over the years.

Barb shot her a glare. 'No, you won't,' she said. 'I'm tired of people speaking for me. It's like this, Zal. I've got something called alopecia. My hair has been falling out, which is obviously not great when I'm supposed to be a hair content creator.' She spat the last few words out as if they were poison. 'And as if that wasn't enough, I've discovered that my mother is alive and my aunt has been lying to me about it all my life.'

Zal gasped and seemed speechless. But only for a moment. His hand found Barb's arm and he squeezed it before saying, 'Shit, Barb. This is more drama than when you were in the Real Residence.'

'You went into the Real Res?' Serena's jaw had officially fallen on to the table.

'But seriously,' interrupted Zal, his face dropping into a look of concerned sadness. 'Are you OK, Barb? How did you find out?'

'She sent me a message on ShowReal when I went quiet, to check I was OK. But it turned out that Jess had discovered she was alive, and thought I knew and that I had been lying about her being dead all my life. So she's only just started talking to me again after a long period of what I'm going to describe as silence.'

Zal nodded slowly.

'But the main thing is that I've made a decision. I can't live trapped in that flat any more with nothing but a dwindling number of followers on ShowReal.'

'Hardly,' shot back Serena. 'You've still got several hundred thousand.'

'Whatever. The numbers have started to become completely meaningless to me, really. They don't actually bear any relation to my real life. And I don't want to live like this any more, obsessing over how many likes I've got or how many shares. I don't want the world outside to be nothing more than a dream.'

Barb looked at Serena. 'When you're an influencer, creator, *whatever* you want to call it, nothing is ever enough. A quarter of a million followers, half a million, a million – the numbers get bigger and bigger but the sense that you're actually achieving anything gets smaller and smaller. All this time I've thought that I was this bad person, responsible for my mother's death. A burden on my aunt. That the only good thing about me was my bloody hair.'

With this, Barb whipped off her hat. Serena gasped.

'Can I just let it be known here,' Zal said, 'that I have never given a shit about your hair, given that I cannot actually see it.'

'Thank you for saying that, Zal,' continued Barb. 'You know, you're the one who has made me think about what I'm doing with my life. I'm going to be seventeen in a couple of weeks and I've finally worked out what actually matters. It's not looking good or having great content or some banging career. None of those mean anything if you're literally having to destroy yourself to get them. Do you know what matters?'

Serena looked blank.

'Weetabix?' suggested Jess, waggling her eyebrows.

'Well yeah, obviously Weetabix matters.' Barb smiled at her friend. 'But what really, really matters is living in the *truth*. And I don't give a toss how cheesy that sounds.'

'Cheese tastes pretty damn good.' Zal nodded. 'Couldn't live without it.'

'Right. Cheese it is,' said Barb firmly. 'And I've got a plan. I just need you guys to help me with it.'

They sat spellbound. And she told them *exactly* what she wanted to do.

CHAPTER 19

Barb lay in bed thinking. She had never had a birthday party before. As a small child, she had learnt not to ask for one. The one time she had suggested it just before her fifth birthday, Sorcha had actually laughed. Who would she invite? A party needed people and Sorcha had ensured that there weren't many of those in Barb's young life.

Barb thought of all the birthdays that had passed unmarked by her mother. All the chances she had to send a card, or get in touch and reveal the truth. Gone, because of what? Drugs?

Today, on the occasion of her seventeenth birthday, Barb still hadn't had all that many people to invite. But she had enough. And the number in attendance wasn't really what mattered: it was about the quality of the party, not the quantity of people who walked through the door. As a child, Barb had seen her lack of friends, her lack of popularity, as a sort of reflection of her quality as a human being. But it had not been that. It had not been anything more than a reflection of her circumstances, circumstances she had had no part in creating herself. Circumstances that had been pushed on her by Sorcha and Orla.

She had spent the past month putting her plan in place. The venue was easy. The Secret Garden had agreed to give her the pub free of charge in exchange for exposure on social media – and Barb was pretty sure she could keep her side of the bargain on this occasion.

Some people had been invited without knowing what was going to happen. Being deceitful wasn't Barb's thing – even if it did seem to run in the family – but she had needed to tell a few fibs to be able to really pull off her plan. Anna G fell into that camp – Barb had sent the invite alongside a tantalising email threatening to blow the lid on the Real Residence. Barb didn't like having to do that . . . but needs must. Caz and Juan didn't need to be told the reason for a party – an invitation was enough to ensure their attendance.

Pixie knew exactly what Barb had up her sleeve, having been in touch to apologise for everything that had gone on in the Real Res. Amy was also on board, sending a number of clapping emojis when she had received the message. Zal, Jess and Serena were obvious attendees, as was Pete.

There were just two other people that Barb needed to invite. For many days she wasn't sure she could. She was angry, and she also wasn't sure if she was ready to see them. But deep down, she knew her plan wouldn't come off without at least one of them there to see it. To learn just how much power she had inside her after all those years without it.

Barb sent a WhatsApp to Sorcha.

And a nervous reply to Orla online.

The thought of actually meeting her mother filled Barb with a queasy mix of hope and trepidation. For what seemed like hours, Barb stared at the message and waited for it to go from 'delivered' to 'seen'. Then she breathed deeply as she watched the words 'typing' on the screen.

@OfficialO: 'I would be honoured to come to your seventeenth birthday party, and I want to say what a generous thing this is for you to do, Barb.'

Even if she didn't turn up, it would be OK. Barb had lived this long without her, after all.

Jess stuck her head around the bedroom door. 'You ready to start that outrageously good life of yours?' she asked, grinning.

'I've never been readier for anything,' said Barb. And she meant it.

* * *

266

Zal, Serena and Jess got there early to help set up. In truth, they didn't need much but a tripod to prop the camera phone up and a few bags of crisps to serve as party food. The snacks and drinks and decorations weren't really the point of *this* party, while the dress code was 'Come as you are'. They hadn't bothered to get dressed up or put make-up on for the occasion. Barb was wearing jeans, a T-shirt and her trusty beanie even though the temperature had soared.

This was what Barb was: a slightly awkward teenager with alopecia who was finally feeling comfortable in herself.

And while she would have been lying if she'd said she wasn't nervous, she still couldn't summon any jolts despite the enormity of what lay ahead: just the same strange calm that she had experienced when she found that first patch, which had now spread over almost her entire head. Just a few straggles of long, golden hair remained here and there.

She twirled one that had come loose from her beanie around her index finger now as she waited for the guests to arrive.

Caz and Juan came first, keen as mustard. Then Pixie, who looked bright-eyed and clean, trailed by Amy, who enveloped Barb in a huge bear hug. 'You don't need extensions, babes,' she said, grinning widely at Barb. 'You're beautiful just as you are. You've got a sparkle that most certainly wasn't there when I last saw you.'

Anna G was *not* happy when she walked through the door to the dingy pub. 'This had better be good!' she trilled, before asking the barman what champagne they had. Pete joined her at the bar and suggested a good ale, which left Anna G so shocked she was actually stunned into silence. 'Pork scratchings?' he continued – Barb thought Anna was going to faint clean on to the floor.

In fact, Barb was laughing so hard that she almost missed the moment that the door swung open and her mother walked in. Her actual, living, breathing mother. She was trailed by a circumspect-looking Sorcha, but even if her aunt hadn't been there, even if Barb had never seen a photo of her mum before, she would have known it was her.

Strangely, Orla's glossy hair had gone too, left lank and limp from years of drug abuse, Barb assumed. She looked tiny, weak, on the brink of defeat.

She was a stark contrast to Sorcha, who had clearly continued to take deliveries from OKHUN even after Barb had left, and was dressed in some Lycra get-up complete with glittery eyeshadow. Her aunt had certainly come as she was: a woman so deeply unsure of herself that she would take on whatever happened to be in fashion at the time, even if it made her look like a Quality Street.

There was a collective intake of breath as Barb walked towards Orla. Everyone could see that they were mother and daughter, even without knowing the story:

'So you really do exist,' said Barb, standing in front of the woman who had given birth to her, the woman she had not, as it turned out, killed by coming out of her womb.

'I'm so sorry,' said Orla, her voice so tiny it shocked Barb.

'It's OK,' replied her daughter, trying her best not to cry. 'You're here now.'

Then Barb, conscious that she needed to stay strong, turned to address the assembled guests at her first ever birthday party.

'Zal, Jess,' she said to her friends (she wasn't counting Serena as one – just yet). 'It's time to start broadcasting live.'

There was a murmur from the general direction of the bar, and a shrieked, 'I DON'T WANT TO BE ON CAMERA!' from Anna G.

Barb turned to her with a sharp look. 'Don't worry, Anna. Nobody is going to be looking at you, believe me.'

Jess went over to the tripod and pressed record on Barb's phone. Zal lifted up his phone and pressed record on that too.

The Secret Garden was now being broadcast live to all of @letdownyourhair's followers and 1.5 m of @IAmZal's.

'Thank you, everyone, for coming,' announced Barb, before clearing her throat. 'It means a lot that you are here, and thank you everyone at home or wherever you are, for watching this now. I promise you won't be disappointed with what you see. I'm just going to wait a bit, to let people get into the live, and then we will be ready to go.'

Anna G looked like a bulldog chewing a wasp. Sorcha's eyebrows were arched almost to the sky. Pixie was smiling and getting out her phone to film too.

Barb soaked up the moment, allowed it to wash over her, aware that, for once, she was completely safe. Nobody there could hurt her. Not any more.

'Right, I think I'm ready.' Jess nodded while Zal gave a thumbs up. 'My name is Barb,' she began. 'Though many of you know me as @letdownyourhair. For a while, people actually used to call me by my handle. I mean, how ridiculous is that? And actually, for a while I thought of *myself* as my social-media profile, nothing more than the girl you saw making loads of videos about how to have perfect hair. And you know, that's fine. There's loads of space for people making videos about how to have perfect hair, or make-up, or clothes, or life. Social media is full of those accounts. You only have to open up ShowReal and you can't move for them. But I was finding I didn't want to pretend I had a perfect life on social media, because, you know, in the background, *off* social media, my life wasn't perfect. Not at all.' She looked at Sorcha, who winced. 'My entire world was inside my screen and the four walls of my bedroom. I thought that the only thing that mattered was getting likes and more follows and better brand partnerships, so I could earn my keep with my aunt. So I could earn my keep in my own *home*.'

Pete shook his head mournfully. Sorcha shot him a death stare.

Barb forged on, regardless of all the daggers that were being shot back and forth through the room. 'I thought that my hair was the only thing I had going for me,' she said, allowing the words to land. She paused, breathed iiinnn through her nose and outtttt through the mouth. 'But then something happened.' Barb took another deep breath just to make sure she was fully in control.

She looked to Jess for reassurance and Jess nodded at her, mouthing, 'You can do it!'

And there, in front of everyone at the pub and an online audience of almost a million people, Barb whipped off her beanie hat to reveal her balding scalp.

Orla's hands flew to her face as she tried to cover the look of sadness that had grown across it.

Anna G gasped and downed her ale in one. Pete winked at her.

Jess gave Barb a thumbs up. Unbeknownst to Barb, the viewing figures were going up and up and up.

'My hair started falling out, as you can see. I got alopecia. Now, I thought alopecia made me a freak because guess what? I didn't see anyone with this on my social media. I only saw perfection. Beautiful hair, beautiful skin, beautiful, perfect lives. And I felt awful. But then something even weirder happened, The more my hair fell out, the more I realised what actually mattered. And it wasn't likes or follows or filters. It wasn't having glossy, wavy hair. It was being me.'

Barb paused, sure that she had just seen a tear fall down her aunt's perfectly made-up face. 'You know, social media doesn't need more people telling you how to have a perfect life. It needs more people telling you how their lives are *really*, how it's OK to have an *imperfect* life. It needs more people normalising their flaws, because guess what? Being imperfect, being a screw-up, it's nothing to be ashamed of.' She looked pointedly at her mum and her aunt. 'It's not something to lie about, to try and hide out of view, because doing that just makes things worse. Believe me, I know. And so now I want to be honest with you all. I want you to see the real me, the person behind @letdownyourhair.'

Serena stepped forward and handed Barb an electric razor. Anna G knocked over Pete's pint in shock. Pixie clapped her hands together and Amy let out a whoop. Sorcha squealed a strangled 'no!'. Caz and Juan stared daggers at their colleague, their eyes telling her to shut up.

And Orla . . . well, Orla smiled at her.

Meanwhile, Zal and Jess continued filming, tears in their eyes.

Barb looked at the machine in her hand, then raised it to her head. She turned it on. And in front of an audience of two million people, she finally, truly, let down her hair.

AUTHOR'S NOTE

Let Down Your Hair is, of course, based on the fairy tale of *Rapunzel*. But it is also based on my own experiences of losing my hair as a teenager. When I was eighteen, I developed Alopecia areata. My sister found it while she was straightening my hair one afternoon – a smooth patch no larger than a five pence piece. I wouldn't have noticed it if she hadn't. But within weeks, it had grown and been joined by other large patches, until my scalp resembled a hodgepodge of hair and skin. I was about to go to university. I was embarrassed and ashamed and believed that it was some sort of punishment for being a bad person. I had suffered from Obsessive Compulsive Disorder since childhood, terrible ruminations that told me I was evil and had probably done terrible things that I had blanked out in horror. I was terrified my family would die and chanted phrases to try and keep them alive. The Alopecia made sense – my outsides finally matching my insides.

Almost twenty-five years on, I have realised that Alopecia is actually more like my body's way of trying to tell me it is suffering. That it needs love and nourishment and help. That it needs a break. We tried all sorts of cures for it, but

I've discovered that in my case, the best treatment is to live the life I am meant to, not the life I *think* I need to. When a patch appears, it reminds me of my true self, hiding under all the hair dye and blow-dries and make-up. That my true self is just as beautiful as any filtered or posed picture I could post on Instagram, and just as worthy of love, likes and shares.

ACKNOWLEDGEMENTS

This book is dedicated to my friend Emma Campbell, who is a gift. I would also like to thank Holly Beck, Giorgie Ramazzotti, Laura Cole and Martha Freud for their enduring love and friendship. Thank you to my mum, dad, sister and brother for always being there even when they had their own stuff going on.

As ever, Nelle Andrew is my sun and stars (and agent, but mostly, my sun and stars). Seven books in ten years . . . and I couldn't have done any of it without you!

At Hachette, I would like to extend a huge thank you to the wondrous Naomi Greenwood, who I have learnt so much from. You made the whole process of creating Barb a joy, and I am very grateful for all your direction and encouragement. Barb, Zal and Sorcha wouldn't exist without you. Thank you to Emily Thomas for being an ace press person, to Beth McWilliams for brilliant marketing and to Alison Padley for the most glorious cover. Thanks also to Ruth Girmatsion and Philippa Willitts for your valuable input.

Thank you to Sophy Silver for all her lessons in TikTok. A huge shout out to Amit Patel, whose campaigning and writing has done so much to inform me about life with a visual impairment. And to Kika, his gorgeous guide dog who accompanied us on our three-hour schlep around south London! I would also like to thank James Rath, whose YouTube content has taught me so much.

I want to express the most endless gratitude to Harry, who holds me through everything. And last, but most certainly not least, I must thank Edie. Every word I write is my tiny attempt at making the world a better place for you.

SUPPORT

Many young people struggle with some of the same issues as Barb including mental health, anxiety, bereavement and depression. Help is out there. For more information on where to find support, advice and help, please look at the following list of amazing charities:

CHILDLINE
A private and confidential service for young people up to age 19. Contact a Childline counsellor about anything – no problem is too big or small. Available 24 hours.
Call free on 0800 1111 or talk online at childline.org.uk

MIND
Offers advice and confidential support to anyone experiencing a mental health problem. Helplines are open 9am–6pm on weekdays except for bank holidays.
Call on 0300 123 3393 or find them at mind.org.uk

THE MIX
Offers advice and confidential support for under 25s, including a crisis messenger. Helplines are open 4–11pm every day and web chat is available 24/7.

Call on 0808 808 4994, text THEMIX to 85258, or find them at themix.org.uk

SAMARITANS
Confidential and emotional support for people who are experiencing feelings of distress, despair or suicidal thoughts. Lines open 24/7 and 365 days a year. If you need a response immediately, it's best to call on the phone.
Call free on 116 123 or find them at samaritans.org

SHOUT UK
Shout is a free, confidential, 24/7 text messaging support service for anyone who is struggling to cope.
Text SHOUT to 85258 or find them at https://giveusashout.org
Text any time for free, to talk with a trained volunteer who'll help you feel calmer.

YOUNG MINDS TEXTLINE
Provides free, 24/7 text support for young people across the UK experiencing a mental health crisis. All texts are answered by trained volunteers, with support from experienced clinical supervisors.
Text YM to 85258.

KT Bruce/Alamy Stock Photo

Bryony Gordon

In the twenty years that she has worked for the *Telegraph*, Bryony Gordon has become one of the paper's best-loved writers. She is the author of the bestselling *The Wrong Knickers* plus *The Sunday Times* Number One bestsellers *You Got This* and *Mad Girl* which were both nominated for British Book Awards. She is the presenter of the *Mad World* podcast and in 2016 she founded Mental Health Mates, now a global peer support network which encourages people with mental health issues to connect and get out of the house. In 2017, she won the MIND Making A Difference Award for her work in changing the perception of mental health in the media. She lives in South London with her husband and daught--- You can follow Bryony on Instagram: @bryonygordon

Gor